D0546610

WHITE FOX
IN THE FOREST

WHITE FOX
IN THE FOREST

Chen Jiatong

Translated by Jennifer Feeley

Chicken House

Scholastic Inc.

If you purchased this book without a cover, you should be aware
that this book is stolen property. It was reported as "unsold and destroyed"
to the publisher, and neither the author nor the publisher has received
any payment for this "stripped book."

Original Chinese text copyright © 2019 by Chen Jiatong
English translation by Jennifer Feeley, copyright © 2021 Chicken House
Interior illustrations copyright © 2021 by Viola Wang

Originally published in hardcover in 2022 by Chicken House,
an imprint of Scholastic Inc.

Published in China as *Dilah and the Wheel of Reincarnation* by Jieli
Publishing House in 2019.
First published in the United Kingdom in 2021 by Chicken House,
2 Palmer Street, Frome, Somerset BA11 1DS.

All rights reserved. Published by Scholastic Inc., *Publishers since 1920*.
SCHOLASTIC, CHICKEN HOUSE, and associated logos are trademarks and/or
registered trademarks of Scholastic Inc.

The publisher does not have any control over and does not assume any
responsibility for author or third-party websites or their content.

No part of this publication may be reproduced, stored in a retrieval system,
or transmitted in any form or by any means, electronic, mechanical,
photocopying, recording, or otherwise, without written permission of the
publisher. For information regarding permission, write to Scholastic Inc.,
Attention: Permissions Department, 557 Broadway, New York, NY 10012.

This book is a work of fiction. Names, characters, places, and incidents
are either the product of the author's imagination or are used fictitiously,
and any resemblance to actual persons, living or dead, business
establishments, events, or locales is entirely coincidental.

ISBN 978-1-338-79404-5

10 9 8 7 6 5 4 3 2 1   22 23 24 25 26

Printed in the U.S.A.   40

This edition first printing 2022

Book design by Stephanie Yang

The adventure so far...

Ever since he was a little fox cub, Dilah had dreamt of becoming human. Then, one day, a day that was forever etched in the Arctic fox's mind, a rival fox named Carl hatched a plot that snatched away both of Dilah's parents. Before she died, Dilah's mother told him about an ancient legend: A long time ago, the patron saint of the Arctic foxes, Ulla, created a secret treasure like no other. Whoever found it would be granted the ability to transform from an animal into a human being, superior to all other living things! Determined to turn his dream into a reality, Dilah set off on a quest to find Ulla's treasure, guided by the precious object that his mother had left him—the moonstone.

On his journey from the Arctic, Dilah made several friends along the way, including a clever weasel called Ankel and a kindhearted rabbit named Little Bean. They joined Dilah on his quest, braving all the adventures that came their way together. Carl, who was now the head of the Arctic foxes, kept close on their trail, eager to get his paws on the moonstone. A bloody battle broke out when Carl tried to steal the moonstone from Dilah. Just when Dilah had lost all hope, his long-lost older brother, Alsace, showed up, driving away Carl and saving the day—or so Dilah thought. In fact, Alsace turned out to be no better than Carl. He stole the moonstone, then imprisoned Dilah and his friends in a cave, threatening to kill them one by one if Dilah refused to reveal the moonstone's secret.

Dilah found himself trapped in the cave alongside Ankel and Little Bean. He'd resigned himself to his fate, when a young female fox appeared in the moonlight at the mouth of the cave . . .

CHAPTER 1

Makarov's Loss

The guard fox snorted awake as the slender female fox approached him, her coat gleaming red in the moonlight. Dilah's ears stood up sharply as he watched from the cave's darkness.

"Miss Emily!" the guard exclaimed, leaping to his feet and shaking out his own red coat in embarrassment. "What are you doing . . . I mean . . . to what do I owe the honor of your presence?" Ankel and Little Bean joined Dilah closer to the entrance, wide-eyed with confusion . . . and a little bit of hope. Who was Miss Emily, exactly, and what was she up to?

"Hello, Michael. Father sent me to relieve you," she said.

"Oh . . . b-but your father, he never mentioned—"

"Oh, it must've slipped his mind," Emily interrupted. "You know what Father's like—his duties as head elder keep him so busy. He knows you're all working so hard too, and wanted to give you a break." Dilah blinked, mesmerized by her enchanting voice.

"Are you sure? Y-you're not often on guard duty, Miss Emily," Michael stammered. "And there are three pri—"

Emily cut him off. "You think I can't handle a puny white fox, a skinny weasel, and a mangy rabbit?" She giggled. "Come on, Michael. You know I'm tougher than that. Now, go get some rest."

The guard appeared to relax. "Thank you, Miss Emily," Michael said, slinking off into the night.

Emily sat quietly at the cave entrance until the guard was well out of earshot. Dilah, Ankel, and Little Bean waited on tenterhooks. What were her intentions? Was she really there to relieve the guard? Then, at last, she turned to the prisoners.

"Dilah?" Emily called.

Dilah stepped warily into the moonlight. "What do you want?"

"There's no time to explain. Hurry up and come with me," Emily said, scampering away from the cave.

The three friends looked at one another in astonishment. Dilah nodded, and they scurried out after their savior, their steps as light as air.

But Dilah's heart sank as he absorbed the scene outside. A small group of foxes blocked Emily's way, sealing off the path down from the rocky cave to the grassy plains. He, Ankel, and Little Bean hesitated a few paces behind. Emily didn't appear to be afraid. In fact, her fluffy tail swished with impatience.

"Miss Emily, you said that you only wanted to have a look at the prisoners," said the fox at the head of the group. "If we let them go—"

"Listen, Frank, you're my servants, all of you. So, blame everything on me. Say that I forced you to do it."

"But—" Frank protested.

"No *but*s. We don't have time for this. Thank you for your loyalty and help over the years. Now, step aside." Although her voice was gentle, it was filled with steel. The small group stepped aside.

Dilah, Ankel, and Little Bean followed closely as they passed through the group and into the night—into freedom.

The moon was half-hidden by dark clouds. A cool breeze rustled the grass, brushing past Emily, Dilah, and his friends as they ran. In the dim, white moonlight, Dilah admired Emily's delicate features. She'd mentioned that her father was the head elder—clearly one of Alsace's trusted foxes. Why would the daughter of the head elder risk her life to save complete strangers?

The sky grew lighter, ribboned with wisps of drifting clouds, the horizon aglow with the orange glimmer of dawn. They ran nonstop for hours, until they were out of breath and barely able to continue.

Emily slowed to a walk and finally to a blissful halt

by a small trickling stream that flowed down from a mountain range in the distance. Once the animals had drunk their fill, Emily spoke. "We should be safe here, for now."

Dilah stepped forward. "I'm glad you rescued us, Miss Emily. But . . . *why* did you rescue us?"

"Because I'm joining your quest, of course! And please, none of that *Miss Emily* nonsense. *Emily* is fine."

"Sorry . . . What?" Ankel said.

Little Bean hopped confusedly from foot to foot.

"I said, you can call me—" Emily started.

"No, before that," Dilah interrupted quietly. "You said you're . . ."

"I'm joining your quest."

"But why?" said Little Bean, bouncing over.

"Because I want to. And besides, I have the moonstone!" Emily triumphantly declared, lifting her head to display Dilah's beloved leather parcel dangling around her neck.

Dilah stared at the parcel in awe, shocked and delighted in equal measure. They'd escaped from the cave, they'd recovered the moonstone, *and* they had a new companion!

"How'd you pull that off?" he asked, grinning.

"I stole it from Alsace," Emily said proudly, smiling back at Dilah. "He's so full of himself, he didn't think anyone would dare."

"But *why* do you want to join us?" Ankel asked, eying her suspiciously. Clearly he wasn't quite as delighted as Dilah. And perhaps he had a point. Why would Emily surrender a comfortable life and betray her friends and family for the chance of . . . what? "This isn't a game. Do you realize how dangerous this is?"

Emily's eyes flashed angrily. "Of course I realize how dangerous it is, you patronizing little worm! I've given this a lot of thought. I've lived with the fox clan long enough. I'm sick of being little 'Miss Emily.' I want to see the world. I want to make a difference! And I want some actual respect, if that's not too much to ask. Is that a good enough reason for wanting to join you?"

Ankel bowed his head sheepishly as Dilah spluttered a laugh.

"Welcome to our group!" Little Bean said with a warm smile.

"Yes—we're glad to have you," Dilah added slowly, turning over his thoughts carefully. "But . . . Ankel's right about one thing: Treasure hunting's no walk in the park. I don't mean any disrespect, Emily, but it's far less comfortable than what you're used to."

"No problem! My mind's made up!" Emily firmly declared. "Now, we should probably get going. We don't want to give them a chance to catch up. But first . . ." Carefully, she lifted the moonstone from around her neck and offered it to Dilah.

He accepted it, relieved to feel its weight around his neck once again. Just like that, Dilah's treasure-hunting team had a new member. Still, he couldn't help but be wary of Emily's sudden appearance and apparent selflessness. It didn't make sense to him. If she simply wanted to see the world, there was no need for her to betray the other foxes in her clan. Could it be that she too was entranced by the ancient legend, the promise that at the end of the moonstone's path, an animal could be transformed into a human? Or did she have some other motive?

"So . . . where to next?" Dilah asked, gazing doubtfully far into the distance. Beyond the grassy plains, a never-ending mountain chain merged with the blue sky. Mist curled around the snowcapped peaks.

"That doesn't look like an easy route," said Little Bean.

Ankel glanced around. "But is there any other way, if we want to lose Alsace?"

Emily smiled. "Ankel's right—that's where we have to go. It takes almost a week to get around those mountains up ahead . . . but I know a shortcut. There's a small path that cuts straight through, and I'm pretty sure no one else in Alsace's clan is aware of it. Once we reach the forest beyond the mountains, we'll have ditched them!"

"Emily, lead the way!" Dilah said.

—◦—

Hours later, they reached a pass between two mountains. As promised, Emily's route was well hidden—but she clearly knew the terrain like the back of her paw. The path was strewn with rubble, sharp rocks jutting out on either side. As they climbed higher and higher, Dilah's, Ankel's, and Little Bean's footsteps grew heavier.

"C'mon! We're getting close!" Emily didn't seem tired at all. She bounded ahead, cheering them on as they trudged up the slope, zigzagging around boulders. "And to think, *you* were worried about *me* being too soft for adventuring!" She giggled.

Blushing under his fur, Dilah picked up the pace.

Finally, they came upon a gigantic ravine between the two mountains, the sides so steep they couldn't see the bottom.

"All we have to do is jump across," Emily said brightly. "And from then on, it's easier. Come on, I'll show you where the gap is narrowest." The path grew steeper and narrower. Emily carefully crawled along, close to the mountain wall, as Dilah and the others nervously trailed behind, half crouching and half climbing to make sure they kept their balance. No one dared utter a peep. The only sounds were the crunching of stones beneath their paws and the pitter-patter of their hearts.

Suddenly, behind Dilah, Ankel cried out and slipped, plunging a few pieces of rubble into the abyss below, his foot hanging over the ledge. He clung to the path, panting, as Little Bean and Dilah carefully helped him up. Dilah listened for the rubble hitting the bottom of the ravine, but it felt like ages before the dull echo rang out.

"Are you OK?" Dilah asked. Ankel bit his lip and nodded, shooting a mistrustful glance at Emily where she stood watching a few paces ahead.

After nearly an hour of this difficult trek, they finally reached the narrowest crossing point and, one by one, leapt the small gap over the ravine. Dilah allowed his heart rate to slow as they perched high atop the neighboring mountain, surveying the other side of the range. A forest stretched on and on like a vast green ocean, lush and vibrant.

And a forest meant *food*! Dilah's stomach rumbled in anticipation.

"Come on!" Emily said, catching Dilah's eye. "I'm starving too!"

Together, Dilah and Emily bounded down the

mountainside, Little Bean and Ankel following, hooting and hollering. At one point, Little Bean lost his balance and fell on his bottom. But it was all right—he coasted down the mountain on his fluffy backside as though he were riding a sled! When he reached the valley floor, he jumped up and rubbed his hindquarters, laughing gleefully.

As soon as they entered the forest, they started foraging for food. Ankel found hazelnuts and mushrooms, Emily discovered all sorts of wild fruits, and Dilah caught a large salmon from a nearby stream. Little Bean busied himself with finding the perfect place to eat.

At last, they settled down beneath a huge tree to feast until their bellies were full. When night came, the moon shone brightly through the trees onto the grass, casting mottled white shadows, the forest echoing with the drawn-out cries of birds getting ready to sleep. Ankel, Little Bean, and Emily curled up beneath a tree and appeared to fall asleep quickly, but Dilah tossed and turned on his bed of leaves. Despite the big meal in his stomach and the safety of his friends nearby, he felt restless, his eyes wide open.

As he stared up at the crescent moon, he decided it was

time to seek guidance from the moonstone again. Afraid of waking up his friends, he crept through the bushes to a nearby clearing, where a pheasant darted out of the undergrowth and flew off.

Dilah was about to unwrap the leather parcel around his neck, when he heard footsteps behind him and whirled around. But it was only Ankel. "You're still up?" Dilah asked, surprised.

"With all that's happened lately, I had a hard time sleeping," Ankel said with a grin. "I guessed what you might be up to," he added, nodding toward the parcel.

"You're just in time," Dilah said, removing the parcel from around his neck and opening it beneath the moonlight.

Inside, a large blue gemstone with a golden crescent moon in the center radiated a slowly revolving light. As Dilah and Ankel watched, the small crescent moon started spinning. After a few moments, it slowed to a stop, an arrow pointing in the direction of Ulla's treasure. Following its line, Dilah gazed into the distance between the trees, wondering how much farther they had to travel.

"Look!" Ankel softly cried out. He nudged Dilah, then pointed his snout down at the quivering moonstone.

Dilah stared at the crescent moon in awe. The moon engraving in the stone . . . It was different. Brighter. In all his months of traveling, he'd never seen it so bright!

"Wow! What do you think it means?" Dilah breathed.

"Well . . . maybe Ulla's secret treasure is close by?" Ankel suggested, his voice tight with hope.

"Do you really think so?" The two friends stared at one another, eyes glowing. After traveling for so long, they could finally be nearing the end of their journey.

Snap. Withered leaves crackled in the dense bushes.

"Who's there?" Dilah hissed, whipping his head to face the noise. Had someone been watching? An enemy? Dilah growled at the bushes as Ankel rushed to wrap up the moonstone, its light extinguished by the leather binding.

The forest fell deadly silent. As Dilah's eyes adjusted, he saw a pair of glowing green eyes peering suspiciously at them through the branches and leaves. Scared out of his wits, clutching the moonstone to his chest, Ankel drew in a breath. He appeared to be on the verge of letting out a bloodcurdling scream.

"Come out!" Dilah ordered, stepping in front of his friend.

"Dilah, it's me," a familiar voice called out. The creature stepped out from the bushes: Emily. The suspicious expression in her eyes had disappeared completely, and her face was now unreadable. Ankel let out his breath in a huge, relieved huff.

"What're you doing here?" Dilah asked.

"When I woke up, you all were gone. I was worried something had happened to you, so I came to check," Emily said calmly.

"Why were you hiding in the bushes?" Ankel asked, bristling, apparently recovered from his fright.

"You had your backs to me, and it was dark. I wasn't sure who you were," she explained.

Ankel raised an eyebrow.

"All right," said Dilah, "so it was just a misunderstanding. Let's head back." He hung the moonstone around his neck and turned in the direction of their campsite.

"Wait," said Emily. "Aren't you curious to see where the moonstone is leading?"

"We can do that in the morning," said Ankel. "We should get some sleep."

"But it was glowing brighter, right?" Emily turned toward Dilah. "Don't you think there could be something *really* close by?" Emily sniffed the air. "I don't know about you, but I smell an adventure!"

Dilah's face brightened. He glanced at Ankel. "You go back, if you want."

The two foxes headed though the forest in the direction the moonstone had indicated. Ankel trailed behind, lost in thought, his tiny paw covering his mouth as he gently gnawed on the claw of his index finger . . .

Before long, the trees became thinner and thinner, and they found themselves nearing the foot of what appeared to be a volcano that had erupted long, long ago. The ground was littered with black volcanic rocks. As they approached, Dilah noticed how peculiarly shaped the rocks were: Some stood tall and perfectly straight like plants, a few were huddled over like small animals, while others resembled larger beasts baring their fangs and brandishing their claws. Had all of these creatures been caught in the volcano's path?

"How horrible!" Dilah said.

Then Dilah's sensitive nose caught a whiff of a familiar scent—possibly another fox, but he couldn't be sure.

"Do you smell it too?" Emily asked, sniffing the air.

"I'm not sure, but I think there might be foxes nearby," Dilah replied.

"What?" Ankel twitched in fear.

"Don't worry—it's not Carl or Alsace," Dilah said. "This is a fox we haven't encountered before."

The smell grew stronger and stronger as they crept forward cautiously. After a while, a large black rock appeared, different from the others along the path. Unlike the plant and animal forms, the rock was tall and flat, with a small arched gap at the bottom. A white form was wriggling through the gap toward the friends.

"Wait here," Dilah whispered to Ankel.

Dilah and Emily slowly approached the form, and soon Dilah recognized an Arctic fox. He had a large build, but he'd lost at least half of his fur. The remaining fur was a mess, matted and clumped with twigs and dust. His bare skin was speckled with scars, his bald tail crusted with ringworm scabs. He sat on the ground in front of the odd, tall rock, focused on eating a rotting crow carcass, black feathers strewn across the dirt.

"We'd better stay away," Ankel hissed, frowning, from behind Dilah and Emily.

"Don't be silly, come on!" whispered Emily. "Maybe he

knows something." The ragged fox, sensing movement behind him, turned toward the trio. He leapt to his paws, glaring at the newcomers. The stench from his body and that of the mangled crow were suffocating. Dilah took a few steps back, holding his breath. But what was more disturbing was the expression of shock and recognition on the stranger's face.

"Nicholas . . . you're . . . you're alive?" he said, his voice rough and hoarse.

Nicholas. Dilah remembered the name—he'd been the patriarch of the white foxes in Mama's tale of Gale and Blizzard. Then the stranger's eyes slid over Dilah's face. "No, no, no . . . you're a far cry from him! A far cry . . ."

"Who are you?" Dilah asked gently.

"Who am *I*?" the Arctic fox repeated, his eyes blank. "Oh, right, who am I?"

"What're you doing here?" Emily asked stridently.

"Who are all of you?!" the fox suddenly bellowed, growling.

Dilah stepped a little closer, shooting a glance at Emily.

This conversation needed a soft touch. "My name's Dilah. I'm from the North Pole. These are my friends." He spoke lightly.

"Dilah? Never heard of you," the fox muttered, confused.

"Just now, you called me Nicholas. Do you know him?"

"What did you say? Have you seen him?" the fox excitedly asked, then he hung his head slowly as his memory appeared to return. "No, that's impossible. You can't have seen him. My child is . . . He's . . ." He shook his head, his eyes welling up with tears. "Leave me alone," he said, and turned to walk away.

"Your child? Nicholas is your child?" Dilah called.

The old fox hesitated but didn't reply. Dilah searched his memory for everything he'd been told about Nicholas and the white foxes' complex system of leadership.

"You're Makarov, the second elder of the Arctic foxes," Dilah said. "Isn't that right?"

The crazed fox turned to face Dilah again, apparently stunned into silence. He cleared his throat. "Makarov," he said in a hoarse croak.

"Second elder?" Ankel asked. "What does that mean?"

Dilah and Emily both opened their mouths to reply, but instead, the elder drew himself up straight and started to speak in a low, measured tone.

"The leadership of Arctic foxes is divided in this way: The patriarch oversees the entire clan. The head elder convenes and presides over meetings and safeguards the moonstone, a treasure that's been handed down among generations of foxes. The third elder is responsible for migration, disaster relief, and food distribution. The fourth elder commands the army. But the second elder . . ." His eyes gleamed, and he appeared suddenly like a much younger, sharper fox. "The second elder's job holds the most mystery and danger. They collect information and protect secrets, and also handle the toughest cases in the fox clan. We second elders know the most and thus are particularly vulnerable to ambushes and assassinations, and so we must be highly skilled."

Dilah, Ankel, and Emily blinked at one another in astonishment.

Makarov continued. "It's good to see some foxes after

so long. How are all the white foxes doing?" he asked Dilah. "Arthur's probably the highest-ranking one now. I suppose he took over after Nicholas?" Arthur was Dilah's father and had been ordered by Gray, the head elder, to protect the moonstone.

Dilah swallowed. How long had this fox been lost in the wilderness? "Actually . . . Carl is the patriarch now."

Makarov shook his head in apparent shock. "He actually did it. Carl's always been ambitious. He and Arthur are war heroes, of course—but the status never turned Arthur's head. Carl was different . . . but I never thought he'd go so far."

"Second Elder, why'd you leave the fox clan?" Dilah asked.

The old fox's eyes grew serious and sad. "As you know, my son, Nicholas, was the patriarch, while I served as second elder. He led the white foxes to victory over the blue foxes, driving the blue foxes out of the Arctic Circle entirely and securing his status among the fox clan. Carl, who was known as Gale, and Arthur, who was called Blizzard, helped him win that crucial battle and were hailed as great heroes. But if not for Nicholas, the white foxes would've been wiped out by the war with the blue foxes. My son's contributions to the fox community and the entire species were huge . . . I worked hard to bring him up, giving up so much, watched him fulfill his potential . . . and in the end, all I got was . . . was a dismal death note. Oh, oh! Oh!" Makarov roared wildly, his strong body shaking violently, his limbs beating the ground.

Dilah stumbled backward into Ankel, unsettled by Makarov's sudden change in temperament.

Emily shook her head. "A death note? What do you mean?" she asked gently.

Makarov slumped down. Moments later, he glared up at Dilah and Emily, a strange expression in his eyes.

"What're all of you doing here?" Makarov asked, squinting at the leather parcel dangling in front of Dilah's chest. "Have you come all this way from the Arctic in search of Ulla's secret treasure, just like my son?"

Dilah blinked. Nicholas had been after the treasure too? "We—"

Before Dilah could finish, the second elder rushed toward him at an astonishing speed, snatching the moonstone from around his neck. The old fox was quicker than he looked!

"Hey!" said Dilah, growling, ready to give chase.

But Makarov didn't run away. Instead, he laid the parcel on the ground and opened it, rays of ghostly blue light shooting out from the moonstone, shining on his unkempt face.

"This is it! This is it! It's really it. The moonstone!" Makarov let out a thunderous roar, gasping, his chest heaving. "You fools! You fell for the lies and are trying to track down that evil, bloodstained, unlucky treasure!" He avoided the moonstone's light as though it would burn him.

"Evil, bloodstained, and unlucky?" Dilah was even more confused now.

Ankel edged forward. "What do you mean by that, Makarov?"

"Listen, young fox," Makarov started, fixing Dilah with his bloodshot eyes. "The secret treasure you seek is cursed by Ulla. Whoever possesses it will suffer a fatal disaster. Every hero in historical records who is rumored to have found it or possessed it died mysteriously shortly afterward, without exception. Mark my words, none of you who seek the treasure will come out of this quest alive."

Makarov's warning possessed a kind of cold magic, each and every word deeply etching itself into Dilah's heart. His fur stood on end, and he found himself completely speechless.

The sun had started to rise, and in the eerie silence, a crow swooped down from the red-washed sky and perched atop the huge rock, screeching and fixing Dilah with a deathly stare. It felt like an omen. What if Makarov was right?

Emily broke the silence first. "Impossible! That doesn't make sense!"

Her words snapped Dilah to his senses, his shock fading. "Why would Ulla place such a curse on the fox clan? To curse the offspring that the foxes are supposed to protect?" he asked.

Ankel nodded thoughtfully. "It's hard to believe that Ulla would curse his own followers."

Makarov barked out a laugh. "Foolish weasel. It's actually genius! The secret treasure is bait. Those who believe the rumors and want to search for the treasure are greedy opportunists who'll stop at nothing to achieve their goals. As such, Ulla created a marvelous way to quietly eliminate the dangerous elements in the fox clan and maintain stability." Dilah couldn't help but think of Carl—what Makarov said did have the ring of truth. Had Dilah really gone to all this trouble to search for a treasure that was actually nothing more than a cruel death? A trap for the power hungry?

Dilah shook his head, trying to think logically. "If that's the case, then why do tales of the moonstone and Ulla's treasure keep resurfacing? Why didn't these rumors disappear after the first bad foxes died?"

"There are always more bad foxes, little one. The moonstone automatically returns to the fox clan after completing its mission. The bloodthirsty treasure reappears every time the previous adventurers die, silently waiting to send a new group of opportunists to their deaths."

Dilah lifted his chin. "Not everyone who seeks the treasure is a power-hungry opportunist! Some follow the legend of Ulla out of hope, a desire to make things better. If we find what we seek, we could change the world. Surely Ulla recognizes that?"

Makarov let out another of his strange, hoarse laughs. "Can't you see? How many unknown heroes and villains have fought to the death for this broken stone and the treasure it leads to? Some of them would have been good foxes, like you," he said, now glaring at the moonstone as it caught the sunlight, glowing red. "Like my son. Blood flows like water to feed its power. *That* is why it's cursed."

Dilah was silent. His belief in Ulla's treasure had been dealt a severe blow. The less he wanted to believe Makarov's words, the more they made sense to him.

"Like your son, you said," Ankel ventured. "*This* is how Nicholas died?"

Emily's ears quivered with curiosity.

The old fox took a deep breath. "One day, Nicholas came to me, beside himself with joy, and said, 'Father, I've been investigating our patron saint's secret! I've decided to go and conquer it.' He set out from the Arctic accompanied by an underling, in spite of the opposition of the elders. During the year after he left, I suffered a lot, constantly worrying about his safety, waiting anxiously, until one day, the underling came back, mortally wounded. As soon as he handed Nicholas's note to me, he stopped breathing. No one knows what truly happened to them. By the time I opened the letter, paws trembling, Nicholas had already been dead for weeks."

"What did the letter say?" Emily asked.

Makarov wordlessly walked to the foot of the arch and dug up a piece of worn-out leather, which he dropped in front of Dilah. "See for yourself."

Everyone concentrated on the piece of leather. The writing was blurred by wind and rain, but nevertheless, they could still make out the neat, confident symbols. Perhaps Nicholas's elegant writing was a clue to his mind-set at the time.

Dearest Father,

By the time this letter reaches you, I hope you're still in good health. I miss you very much.

Please forgive my sudden goodbye. I regret that I won't be able to receive your patient guidance anymore. I shall die soon, and perhaps by the time you receive this letter, I'll no longer be in this world.

You must be wondering why I've written this letter. When I left the Arctic, I was already prepared to die to discover the truth of Ulla's legend. I wanted to confirm that legend with my own life. I'm not doing this solely for myself: If the stories and historical sources are to be believed, I must take this step—otherwise, I fear no one else will. I know you'll be sad upon reading this letter, and I'd also like to apologize for my selfish behavior. I have not done my duty to you as a son, and for that I beg for your forgiveness, and for you to forget that you ever had a son like me.

I'll always love you,

Nicholas

Dilah lifted his head to meet the old fox's eyes. He wasn't sure what to make of the letter. It wasn't straightforward, by any means. Nicholas had been prepared to die, but did he? "Is it possible that Nicholas became human?" he suggested.

"Impossible! I knew Nicholas better than anyone. I raised him. If he'd become human, he'd have come back for me, as long as I was still breathing . . . That's why I came here, to a place as close as I knew to the end of his journey. But in all the years I've waited, he's never returned—in fox or human form. He is gone. I know it."

Dilah felt himself plunging into despair. If even a fox like Nicholas had failed, with all his experience and power, what hope did Dilah have of succeeding?

"I'll never see my child again!" Makarov sobbed, suddenly overcome. "Ulla, you stole my only child!"

He threw himself against the huge volcanic rock with a thud. Everyone stared, dumbfounded, afraid to stop him. A moment later, he slowly sank down the slippery stone wall, blankly staring off into the distance. He started to mumble under his breath about food and Nicholas and the moonstone . . . "I'll find you," Dilah deciphered from his incoherent rambling. "Someday, I'll find you."

Dilah and Emily exchanged a glance. The old fox had retreated into his madness. Dilah carefully wrapped up the moonstone and replaced it around his neck, glancing at Makarov one last time before he turned away.

To think that this fox had once helped rule over the Arctic. Now look what had become of him!

"Let's go," Dilah said, his tone serious. The three friends walked off into the dawn.

———◇———

They retraced their way to the campsite in silence. Makarov's words and the letter had shaken the group to the core. Despite the warm sunlight, the forest unfurling all around, a shadow hung over them, and the air was tinged with an unsettling chill.

Dilah's mind was a jumble of mixed-up thoughts. He felt a dull ache in his stomach, as though he'd swallowed a bunch of caterpillars with wriggling antennae. *Ulla's curse . . . the bloodthirsty treasure . . .* These blasted words kept circling in his mind. Makarov's warning pulsed in his ears, the words gnawing at his will like a moth. He didn't want to believe that what Makarov had said was true, but it all felt oddly persuasive. It was as though death were a fanged spider, unfurling its web and quietly awaiting them, luring them in with a dazzling, enticing treasure right in the middle of the web.

Finally, they reached the big tree—with Little Bean enjoying a nap under its boughs—and Ankel volunteered to gather some breakfast. Dilah and Emily woke the snoozing rabbit and filled him in on everything that had happened. He blinked in surprise, scratched his floppy ears in puzzlement, but sat quietly, absorbing the story. When they'd finished, he said philosophically, "Well . . . the old fox has certainly given us a lot to think about."

As Ankel returned with berries and nuts, the foursome settled down to eat. "The thing is . . . what Makarov said is completely different from what Mama implied just before she died," Dilah said hesitantly. "And Mama knew the story from Papa, who was close to Nicholas, I think. She said the treasure was magical. She said I should seek it out for myself. She wouldn't have sent me if she thought

I was going to my death. So . . . was Makarov lying? Or were Mama and Papa?"

His mama's words returned to him as he thought back to the terrible day when she had returned from the hunt alone and mortally wounded. *Legend has it that the patron saint of the Arctic foxes, Ulla, created a secret treasure like no other. It contains an incredible magic that can turn animals into humans . . .* Ankel's voice returned him to the present. "There aren't any holes in Makarov's story, plus, he has no reason to lie," he said.

"There is *one* hole—why did Nicholas leave behind that note? It sounded like he knew he was going to die. How did he know that?" Emily pointed out.

"Exactly!" Dilah agreed. Finally, a glimmer of hope. "Why go on a treasure hunt if you know you're about to die?"

"Maybe he thought the treasure hunt would be so difficult that he might die on the road at any time," Little Bean mused.

"So, what did he mean by confirming the legend with his own life?" Dilah asked.

Ankel clearly had an answer on the tip of his tongue. "He meant that if he could find the secret treasure, he could confirm the curse firsthand," he said smugly. "And you know the outcome. He died! He knew he was going to die. All of which proves Makarov's story."

"Why would you go to all that trouble to confirm a legend, knowing that in doing so you would die and not even be able to tell anyone about it?" Emily argued, her eyes flashing. "That makes no sense!"

"I suspect he didn't die but became human," Dilah said.

"Then why didn't he tell his father that directly?" Ankel shot back. "Why did he tiptoe around the subject like that?"

"That's the big question." Dilah was excited now, his mind spinning faster and faster. "Maybe he was afraid of someone else getting hold of the letter?"

Ankel humphed, grudgingly admitting it was a possibility.

Dilah continued. "Nicholas also said something like 'I'm not doing this solely for myself . . . I must take this step—or no one else will.' Remember? It sounds like there's more to it than simply *dying*!"

The four friends pondered this as they digested their food. "Dilah, do you remember when we spoke to Lund?" Ankel asked. "You know, Little Bean's giant rabbit friend?"

Dilah nodded.

"He mentioned the spring of reincarnation. He told us it was in the enchanted forest."

Dilah chewed the inside of his cheek thoughtfully. "Even at the time, I wondered if that was where the moonstone might be leading us, if maybe the spring was the treasure. But Lund really didn't appear to think the spring would kill anyone."

"Perhaps it's a different source of the transformation magic. Why don't we try to find it first?" Ankel suggested.

"And give up our dream?" Dilah huffed.

"No, that's not what I mean. I mean . . . um . . . the spring of reincarnation can also help us fulfill our dream, and it maybe seems a bit safer."

Dilah glanced at Emily. "I don't know . . . I wasn't there when you heard about this spring, but it doesn't sound quite as exciting to me," she said. "But if you're all convinced . . ."

Dilah turned to Little Bean. "What do you think?"

The rabbit's nose twitched. "I think it's a good idea. Finding the spring could be the answer to becoming human, but if it isn't, we still might find something useful. What've we got to lose?"

Dilah sighed. "OK, that's decided . . . but there's just one problem: Does anyone know the way to the enchanted forest?"

CHAPTER 2

A Rainy Night's Funeral

The friends decided to follow the direction the moonstone had pointed toward, hoping to find a clue along the way that might lead them to the spring of reincarnation. But the forest through which they traveled, though it appeared to stretch on forever, didn't feel enchanted in the slightest. As they continued, Dilah and Emily sniffed out the scents of other animals—and even humans from time to time, although the humans seemed to have passed through days previously.

One morning, as sunlight streamed through the mist and between the tree trunks, Dilah and his friends happened upon a dog and an ox who'd stopped a wild boar foraging for food. The wild boar appeared to be irritable, thrashing two long tusks at the others.

"I don't care about your moral beliefs," said the boar. "I just want some breakfast!" He caught sight of Dilah and the others, and his eyes brightened. "Look, some other animals are headed this way. You can try your little speech on them!" The wild boar scurried off.

The dog was a Dogo Argentino, tall with long legs, a slender waist, and a long face crisscrossed with scars and steely eyes. The big brown ox at his side looked weary. One of his horns had broken off, but the other was incomparably sharp.

"Hello, Arctic fox and red fox," the Dogo Argentino greeted them, only acknowledging Dilah and Emily.

Dilah bristled but decided to ignore the dog's rudeness. He didn't want to pick a fight—especially not with a creature who'd obviously survived a number of battles in his life. "Hello. And you are?"

"I used to be a hunting dog, and I still am . . ." the Dogo Argentino deadpanned, "except now I'm a dog who hunts humans."

The ox rolled his eyes. "Don't worry. He's the president of our alliance. His name's Patrick," the ox explained. "I'm John."

"Care to join our anti-human alliance?" Patrick asked.

"'Anti-human alliance'?" Dilah repeated. *What on earth?*

"Yup. An animal organization that's specifically against humans," Patrick said proudly. "We just led an uprising on a ranch, taking out five herders and freeing several horses, dozens of cattle, and hundreds of sheep. It was a huge victory!"

"Wow . . ." Ankel's jaw hung open.

"I've been planning a large-scale hunting campaign," Patrick continued. "Do you foxes want to join us?"

"I'm sorry, but we must be on our way," Dilah said, feeling a little uncomfortable. He had suffered at the hands of humans, yes—but other humans had been kind to him. *Like animals*, he thought, *humans can be good or evil.*

"That's too bad. You look like you could supply us with a lot of might."

"Why are you fighting against humans?" Emily asked, swishing her bushy red tail.

"Humans have committed so many crimes. They need to be punished," Patrick said coldly.

Emily's ears twitched. "What crimes?"

"They're selfish. They enslave and exploit animals who're valuable to them, and base their happiness on animal suffering," Patrick declared.

John bitterly chimed in. "How many animals have been displaced by human invasion? How many animals have gone extinct because of human hunting? My mother toiled away for a farmer her whole life, transporting people and things. But when she got old and couldn't do any more work, the farmer slaughtered her and sold her meat," the ox said softly. "I saw my own sad future in my mother. So, I broke free of the rope, ran through the fence, and escaped to freedom. I met Patrick along the way, and he inspired me. Since then, we've worked together liberating animals and fighting against humans."

"I'm sorry that happened to your mother," Dilah said carefully. "That's terrible. But it could be said that live-stock and humans have a cooperative relationship. Humans feed and house livestock, who in turn provide them with labor and meat."

"Arctic fox, did you escape from a zoo?" Patrick asked sharply.

"No."

"I didn't think so. You're wild, not like the sickly foxes

in captivity. Now, tell me, on your travels from the Arctic, how many humans hurt you?"

Dilah sighed. "Yes, a human killed my family. But humans have also helped me. In fact, if it weren't for a human, I wouldn't have made it here alive." Dilah thought of the woodsman and his family, who had nursed him to health when he was close to starvation. "Not all humans hurt animals," Dilah argued.

"You only think that because you've never witnessed the crimes they've committed," said Patrick ominously.

Dilah's whiskers twitched in annoyance. Hadn't he just explained that his parents had been killed by humans? But he held his temper. "And you have?"

"I was snatched from my mother's embrace when I was very young. I felt so lonely. Fortunately, not long after, my owner brought home a beautiful Braque Saint-Germain hunting dog. She was flawless, with a lovely orange spot on her face. Her arrival completely transformed my life. She was cheerful and optimistic, melting the ice in my heart like the sun, and gradually, she saved me . . ." Patrick's voice grew wistful.

"We grew up together, never leaving each other's sides, and eventually fell in love. My owner trained me to become a super hunting dog with extraordinary endurance, while he neglected her because she was in poor health. Later, she fell and hurt herself after suddenly contracting a serious illness, but our owner ignored her injury and forced her to go hunting, anyway. She was chasing deer but was so weak that one kicked her down. That was the last time I saw her. She died soon afterward."

Little Bean gasped. Ankel shook his head. "How awful," Emily murmured softly. Dilah felt his heart squeezing at what Patrick and John had witnessed.

"Since then," Patrick continued, "my life has been dark, and I've been in mourning. My love was loyal to a fault, but in the end, her owner drove her to her death. I was furious, a time bomb ready to explode. I quietly waited for the right opportunity, and then one day, due to my owner's carelessness, I found my chance. I lunged at him and wounded him fatally.

"We breathe the same air as humans, drink the same

water—all lives should be equal. This world is as much ours as theirs. I believe that no species, not even humans, is superior to others. So, once I ran away, I vowed to punish humans. And I will carry out my anti-human campaign for as long as I live!" Patrick growled.

"But aren't you living in a world of hatred, if killing humans is your goal?" Dilah asked.

"Of course that's not my goal. Our ultimate objective is to build a fair world in which all animals can live freely according to the laws of nature, but before we can achieve that, we have to get rid of humans. That's why I've traveled thousands of miles to establish an anti-human alliance. I want to recruit a huge animal army from the animals in this forest and beyond. Since we can't rewrite history, let's create a new one! Would you like to join us in establishing a new world?"

"I'm afraid we have to respectfully decline. We are chasing after our own dream," Dilah said. "But thank you for telling us your stories."

Bang. A shot rang out from deep in the forest.

"That's too bad, but I respect your decision," Patrick

said. "It's not a good idea to stay in this forest. As you can hear, it's full of hunters. You'd better leave at once."

"We're only passing through," Dilah said, "but thank you. Good luck."

Dilah, Emily, Ankel, and Little Bean turned away.

───◇───

After they'd walked a while, Emily broke the silence. "Dilah, after hearing what Patrick said, do you still dream of becoming human?"

"I want it even more now."

"Why?"

"Because we can only change the cruelty of humans to animals by becoming human," Dilah said, smiling.

Emily nodded her understanding. The tension in the small group lessened slightly as they continued through the forest.

The temperature had dropped little by little, and dark clouds had hidden the sun beyond the treetops. At last, a cool autumn drizzle started to fall. Toads emerged lazily from their holes. There was a feeling of weariness spreading throughout the forest, and as night started to fall, birds returned to their nests between the leaves speckled with yellow, brown, and red, while frogs and crickets croaked and chirped. The friends trudged on.

"The rain's getting heavier, and the wind's picking up—it feels like there's going to be a downpour," Ankel said uneasily, almost tripping over a dazed toad.

Little Bean's nose twitched in agreement. "Let's pick up the pace and try to find shelter in a cave or tree hole before it gets worse."

But the sky grew even darker and there was no shelter in sight. A gust of wind whipped through the forest, blowing the leaves in all directions, a strange sound mingling with the whistling of the wind. Cautiously, they slowed down. "What's that noise?" Emily said, glancing over at Dilah. "Can you smell something too?"

Dilah caught a whiff of an unfamiliar scent but couldn't place it before the wind whipped it from his nose. He was scanning the trees when he realized what it was.

It was the scent of danger, and suddenly Dilah was frozen to the spot with fear.

A man picked his way through the trees nearby,

returning to his home after a hunt. In one hand, he tugged at the leashes of two hounds who were howling up a storm—this was the noise they'd detected under the wind's rustling roar. The hunter carried a small deer on his shoulder and had a shotgun slung over his back. Drizzle whipped his face, and Dilah held his breath, hoping the hunter was too preoccupied with the weather to notice him and the others.

But, catching sight of the small group of traveling animals, the dogs started to bark and strain at their leashes. Dilah trembled, his muscles tensing, and the hunter's eyes shifted until his gaze met Dilah's.

Dilah took a deep breath, his heart in his throat. "Run!" he shouted at his friends.

Emily and Dilah shot off, Ankel and Little Bean following as close as they could over the slippery forest floor.

Eyes gleaming at the sight of a white fox so far from the Arctic, the hunter dropped the carcass of the small deer and chased, his hounds leading the way.

"Look for somewhere with lots of bushes or trees!" Emily instructed, barely breaking her stride.

Bang. A bullet struck the tree trunk beside Dilah, fragments of bark smacking him in the face.

And then the dark clouds finally erupted. Lightning flashed and thunder boomed, the drizzle turning into bean-sized raindrops. The cold rain would wash away their scent, Dilah realized with a little relief; now the hunter and hounds would have to rely on their eyes to track their prey.

Unfortunately for Dilah, his snow-white fur made him stand out among the trees. Instead of dropping behind, the hounds were gaining, and Little Bean and Ankel were struggling to keep up.

Dilah had to do something!

"He's after me," he yelled over the storm. "You guys run the other way!" A bolt of lightning sizzled, and a rumbling sound nearly drowned out his voice.

"I'm not leaving you! If we're going to die, we'll die together!" Emily's entire body was drenched, and for the first time, she looked properly scared.

The hunter was hot on their heels. *Bang!* Ankel slipped on the slick forest floor. Dilah dashed backward and roughly tugged his friend to his feet. The shot had been close, but the weasel wasn't injured. "Come on!" he shouted as Ankel struggled to regain his stride.

Bang! Dilah felt something whizz by his ears as the hounds barked behind him.

The four friends zigzagged around trees, paws slipping on the waterlogged ground, trying to lose the hunter and dogs. As they entered a patch of denser trees, the hunter slowed. Emily led the way into a thicket, where they dove deep, soaking, panting, and exhausted. The hunter hesitated for a moment as he drew near, his dogs struggling to catch a scent in the torrential rain. Darkness had fallen at last, and Dilah allowed himself to hope the man would call off the hunt. But instead, he wiped the rain from his face with his sleeve and scanned the area before settling on the thicket, slowly raising his gun.

He'd guessed where they'd hidden, Dilah realized with dread.

Dilah and his friends shrank backward, shivering, afraid to utter a sound. If they moved, they'd be shot. If they stayed, the hunter would find them, anyway. Despair clenched at Dilah's heart as he felt the weight of the moonstone around his neck. Was this really how it would all end? The hunter waded through puddles, closer and closer.

"Listen! I have an idea, but you must do as I say!" Emily whispered.

"And what's that?" Dilah replied.

"Stay where you are, no matter what, OK?" Emily said gravely. Dilah frowned in confusion. What did she have in mind?

"Wait!" Ankel had realized what she was about to do and stretched out his small paw to catch her, but she'd already darted out of the thicket.

Dilah let out a loud wail as he caught on to Emily's plan. He strained forward, but Ankel and Little Bean held on to him tightly. Emily glanced back through the leaves and reluctantly met Dilah's gaze, thousands of unspoken words shining in her eyes. The moment froze. Then Emily's smile dissolved like mist in the beaded veil of raindrops, and she dashed off toward the hunter, charged with determination.

"It's right there!" the hunter shouted excitedly, and the two hounds lunged at Emily.

Bang. Bang. Two shots were fired, and Emily yelped but carried on running. Dilah felt his heart lift. The hunter must've missed!

The dogs chased, but Emily was nearly impossibly quick on her own, with no rabbit or weasel to slow her pace. She shot through the trees and the rain like a bolt of red lightning.

———◇———

Dilah, Ankel, and Little Bean waited and waited until long after night had fallen, long after the hunter and his dogs had disappeared. The rain continued to pour. Finally, carefully, the three friends emerged from the thicket. "Emily?" Dilah called tentatively. No reply. He tried louder: "Emily!"

They searched for hours for any sign of their friend until at last a small whimper answered their calls. She was lying in a puddle, hidden deep among the roots of a huge, bowed tree. Her red fur had disguised her against the fallen autumn leaves, and the rain had hidden her scent from the dogs. "Emily!" Dilah called, hope rising in his heart.

But when she didn't stir, his hope twisted into dread. His greatest fear was confirmed—as they drew closer, it was clear Emily had been shot. Dilah felt a stab of pain in his chest, as if his heart had torn in two. The wound pierced Emily's flank, and although her chest was still rising and falling, blood was seeping freely from the open gash.

Little Bean was at her side at once, assessing the injury. Dilah knew the rabbit had some knowledge of healing, but despair clenched at his throat as Little Bean lifted his eyes. "Dilah . . . she's dying . . ." Little Bean said, choking back sobs.

Dilah drew closer, bringing his face nearer to Emily's. She blinked slowly. "Dilah . . . I'm so sorry," she said.

"Sorry?" he choked out. Ankel rested a small paw on Dilah's shoulder in support. "You sacrificed yourself to save us. How can you be sorry?"

Emily's eyes flickered. "I've been lying to you, Dilah," she whispered. "Alsace . . . It was his idea for me to free you. He told me to earn your trust . . . find out how to use the moonstone . . ."

Dilah shivered in shock. He glanced at Ankel. The weasel had been right to mistrust Emily, but in the end . . . He shook his head slowly. "Emily, whatever happened in the past, whatever your reasons for joining our quest, you've shown us you're a true friend. You've saved us. But why?"

Emily's bright green eyes were full of tears. "Back in Alsace's clan, I was treated . . . carefully. Others would obey me . . . but only because they feared me and my father. They were always . . . distant. I never had . . . never had a friend." She was struggling to speak, her breath shallow and labored. "But you . . . you all treated me as a friend. You cared for me . . . listened to me . . . trusted me." She blinked a tear from her eye. "And soon, I felt the same. How . . . how could I betray you?" Emily made a choking sound in her throat.

"Thank you, Dilah . . . Ankel . . . Little Bean . . ." Her eyes settled on each of her friends for the briefest moment. "It's been the best time of my life . . ." Emily's breath had grown weaker and weaker, but despite the hammering rain, her voice appeared to Dilah to be the only audible sound in the world.

"Dilah?"

"Mm-hmm." He was holding back a sob.

"Dilah, are you there?"

"Yes."

"Now that you know the truth, do you still consider me a friend?"

"You'll always be my friend, Emily."

"I'm scared. Will you stay with me until I go?"

"Of course."

"I can't see you, it's getting dark . . ."

"I'm here."

"Are you really here?"

"I'm right here in front of you." He rested his cheek against hers.

"Take me with you on your journey . . ."

"I will . . ."

Emily closed her eyes for the last time.

In the pitch-black, rainy night, Dilah, Ankel, and

Little Bean dug a grave for their friend. Lightning tore through the sky, and thunder tumbled over the treetops. At last, the three friends carefully lowered Emily into her grave, hearts overflowing with grief. Emily had been like a shooting star, disappearing after drawing a brilliant arc across the sky of Dilah's life. For the first time, Dilah felt defeated. He couldn't even protect his friend. What good was anything he'd achieved, if he couldn't do that?

They bowed their heads in silence, none of them knowing quite what to say. At last, Dilah spoke.

"We wouldn't have gotten out alive without Emily," he said. "Thank you, friend." He nudged the first scoop of soil onto her body.

———◇———

When Emily was buried, the three friends slept, exhausted, under the half shelter of the tree as the storm blew itself out. When the sun rose, the whole world had changed. Overnight, the leaves had turned the brightest red and yellow, as delicate as flowers in April. The morning dew had settled like pearls, gleaming in the shafts of sunlight breaking through the trees.

When they'd woken and eaten a light breakfast of berries and nuts from nearby, Dilah, Little Bean, and Ankel said their final goodbyes to Emily.

"We should go," Dilah said softly after they'd each spoken a few words, sitting close together by Emily's grave. He couldn't help thinking of his mother; his new grief had painfully opened the old wound of her death. He shook his head, trying to clear his thoughts. If he didn't succeed in his quest to be human, Emily and Mama would have both died in vain. "Let's find the enchanted forest," he said, "and keep a close eye out for hunters. I can't bear the thought of losing anyone else."

CHAPTER 3

The Animal Beauty Pageant

fter another full day of travel and another night on the woodland floor, Dilah, Ankel, and Little Bean finally arrived at the edge of the huge forest. The trees thinned out, but animals abounded, and despite the early hour, they all appeared to be on the move. Sparrows chirped in the branches, flitting from tree to tree in one direction, and flocks of birds flew overhead in an endless stream. Rabbits, minks, wild boars, deer, and even armies of ants followed on the ground, and all appeared to be in high spirits.

"Where are they all going?" Dilah wondered aloud. "Come on, let's follow."

"Are you sure . . . ?" asked Ankel doubtfully. "They can't all be heading for the enchanted forest, can they?"

"It could be important," Dilah objected. "Besides, we don't know where we're headed yet. At such a big gathering, we might meet someone who can point us in the right direction."

"Only one way to find out!" Little Bean said, hopping excitedly from foot to foot.

The three friends followed the animals out of the forest and onto a huge open prairie, bordered by a chain of extinct volcanoes. Dilah's breath caught in his throat— the scenery was so beautiful, he wished Emily were at his side to enjoy it too. Beneath the golden sun, the rippling grass was strewn with layers of yellow, red, and green, shifting in the gentle breeze.

"Come on," said Ankel gently. "We don't want to get left behind!"

They followed the hundreds of animals as they climbed

toward one of the extinct volcanoes, and eventually found themselves at a large, wide-open crater surrounded by smaller craters and trees. The crater basin was dotted with a few larger trees and a small lake in the center, reflecting the blue sky and white clouds. From afar, it looked like a huge blue eye staring up at the sky.

Brightly colored birds soared overhead, exchanging crisp, cheerful cries. The activity on the ground was even livelier: Animals congregated in groups, chatting, discussing, arguing, and even bartering, much to Dilah's bewilderment. Little Bean's long ears quivered in mingled excitement and nervousness as he surveyed the busy scene. But Ankel was overjoyed.

"That's a red deer—do you see the huge antlers on the head of the male? Check out that hazel grouse—the one with the patterned tail—they're very rare!" he explained, captivated. None of the friends had ever seen so many different kinds of animals in one place.

They fell in with a group of animals heading down into the heart of the basin. "A few days ago," a brown bear boomed nearby, "I caught a big sturgeon in the river. It's the tastiest fish I've ever eaten!"

"Oh, that sounds amazing . . . Can you describe it?" the boar next to him asked, drooling.

Voices swirled all around as they reached the central part of the basin, where hundreds, maybe thousands, of animals had congregated.

"My dear old friend, has it been two years since we last met?" a black chicken clucked, affectionately stretching out her wings to embrace another black chicken.

Dilah and his friends weaved their way through the crowd, unsure of what to do. Dilah couldn't help but marvel as he looked around. The other animals also gazed at him curiously. Dilah's white coat really stood out among a sea of brown, black, and gray fur. Many of these creatures had never seen an Arctic fox before.

Among the many curious glances, Dilah felt a pair of eyes glued on him. He turned around to see the boar that Patrick and John had stopped in the forest the previous day. When Dilah met his eyes, he quickly turned his head and pretended not to know him, striking up a conversation with two nearby elk.

"We're not getting anywhere just milling around like this," Ankel pointed out. "We should try to mingle."

He was right. Dilah plucked up the courage and approached a nearby sheep, who was pausing between bites of the grass he was munching with great relish.

"Excuse me. Do you know the way to the enchanted forest?" Dilah politely asked.

"Enchanted?" The sheep opened its mouth in bewilderment, a few blades of grass falling out.

Dilah decided to try his luck elsewhere. "Excuse me. Have you heard of the enchanted forest?" he asked a red deer, who nodded sagely.

"Of course I have. That's a place that fascinates all animals."

"Why is it so fascinating?" Ankel piped up.

"Supposedly, there are all sorts of exotic flowers and plants, as well as all sorts of rare animals, not to mention numerous ancient magic powers. I've also heard there's an enchanted spring. If you drink from it, you'll be cured of all diseases and live forever."

Dilah glanced at Little Bean and Ankel excitedly—he

was probably talking about the spring of reincarnation!

"Where is it? I mean, um, how do we find the enchanted forest?" Ankel asked.

The deer's expression hardened. "I've never heard of an animal who's been able to find it . . . Personally, I don't think it exists at all." The deer glanced over his shoulder. "If you'll excuse me . . ."

"Don't be discouraged, Dilah," said Ankel once the deer had left. "Your hunch was right—the animals here do know something about the enchanted forest. And that was one of the first ones we tried!"

Dilah and his friends continued to talk to animals as they made their way through the crowd, but no one could tell them anything more than the red deer. Eventually, they reached the center of the basin, where a large stage had been constructed out of logs. The animals here were fixated on a performance—a flock of colorful birds singing and swooping in formation over the stage. Dilah stopped and stared transfixed, and when the display was over, he howled enthusiastically along with the hoots, cries, screeches, and flaps of everyone else. An old goat slowly climbed onto the stage and doddered over to a wooden loudspeaker. His face was all skin and bones, in contrast to his large eyes, which were framed by thick bags. A long beard fell to his chest, and a pair of crooked horns sat on either side of his head.

"Thank you! Thank you to the Beetle Bird Troupe for a stellar opening act: 'Autumn Song.' This is the eighth performance of their tour this year. Let's give them another big round of applause." The joyous cacophony started up again. At Dilah's side, Little Bean thumped his feet on the ground and Ankel clapped his little paws. An extra-large smile was pasted across the goat's face as the applause died down.

"Now, let's get to the point. Ahem. We wild animals have been gathering here on the edge of the primeval forest for more than ten years. It's become an annual event. But for those of you who don't know, allow me to introduce myself. I'm Bing, the host of this get-together. Please accept my thanks for your active participation on behalf of the organizing committee." Bing scanned the audience with a practiced eye as the applause started up once again. Once it was quiet, he continued. "As many of you know, we're going to take the opportunity of having so many of you gathered together to hold the third-ever Beauty Pageant of the Primeval Forest. But I have a very exciting announcement: It's going to take place this very afternoon!"

Dilah snorted. *A beauty pageant? What on earth will that involve, across so many species of animals? Ridiculous!*

The old goat continued. "This event only takes place every four years, and the winner will receive a generous prize. Allow me to tell you in advance that the prize this year is very special indeed. The prize is"—Bing stood up on his rear legs, stared with wide eyes, and placed two hooves around his mouth as he dramatically called out—"a map showing the enchanted forest!"

The audience gasped. Dilah, Ankel, and Little Bean glanced at one another in total shock.

The crowd erupted in various murmurs:

"A map showing the enchanted forest?"

"Whoooaaaa, that's wild!"

"It can't be real, surely?"

"Settle down," Bing said. "I can promise you there is no need to question the authenticity of the map—it has been tried and tested. But a word of caution: Animals with a poor sense of direction, you best not try your luck."

Bing peered out from the stage, smiling contentedly at the commotion and confusion.

"So, who wants to give the beauty pageant a try? Are you just itching to join? Are all of you confident and beautiful animals rubbing your paws together in anticipation? Not only is this an opportunity to show off your good looks, but it's also a chance to explore the legendary enchanted forest!" Bing's eyes shone. "Don't be shy—this is the only copy of the map! Members of the organizing committee are waiting for you to sign up. We'll be open all morning, with the primary selection at midday. During the primary selection, we'll determine the contestants, choosing the four most attractive candidates. The final round will take place on the main stage before sundown!"

The crowd roared.

After the animals had begun to disperse, Dilah asked, "What're we supposed to do? We need that map!"

"Why, enter the pageant, of course!" Ankel insisted.

Dilah blinked. "Which one of us?"

Little Bean and Ankel glanced at each other and snorted. "You!" Ankel said. "Silly fox!"

"Me?" Dilah hadn't seen this coming. "How can *I* win?"

"Do you see any other Arctic foxes here?" Ankel said with a serious expression. "Everyone's been admiring your fluffy white coat since you arrived, even though you're covered in dirt. I know you've noticed!"

"Well . . ." Dilah blushed under his whiskers. "I'm not really a performer, though. What do you think I'll have to do?"

Ankel smiled and puffed up his chest. "Don't worry— I'll help you onstage!"

"Are you also going to enter?" asked Little Bean.

"Of course!" Ankel said, his small eyes gleaming. "You never know! We're all beautiful in our own ways. Maybe you should enter too, Little Bean?"

The rabbit flopped his ears down over his eyes

bashfully. "I'd rather not, if that's all right. I don't feel comfortable with this at all."

Dilah didn't feel comfortable either! In fact, he was already squirming with embarrassment at the thought of being paraded up onstage in front of so many onlookers. "Listen, Ankel, isn't there some other way?"

"I'm sorry, but I don't think so. We don't know where the map's being stored, exactly. And there's a lot of security here." He nodded at the burly bears surrounding the stage, their serious expressions indicating their official roles. "So even if we knew where it was, I'm not sure it'd be wise to try to steal it, or even sneak a peek."

"Why don't you join by yourself?" Dilah suggested, feeling panicky as his options narrowed. "Little Bean and I can cheer you on from the audience!"

"No way! We're both entering the pageant. You've got the best chance, Dilah," Ankel adamantly replied. "Trust me. Besides, it might be fun!" He smiled hopefully at Dilah, who softened a little. Ankel's heart was in the right place, as always. It was important to try to win the map, but Ankel was also hoping to distract Dilah and cheer him up. The weasel glanced over at the bright blue lake, where lots of animals were drinking, splashing, or enjoying the sun. "Now, let's go and get ready. We're hardly looking our best after all this traveling!"

———◇———

Ankel spent nearly an hour washing himself meticulously, drying off in the sunshine while obsessively avoiding any dirt, and finally combing the fur on his head until it shone.

Dilah consented to a long swim—it was nice to cool off in the sparkling water and, in the process, clean his fur of the accumulated dirt of hard travel. He felt a deep pang of sadness about Emily, but as he swam, surrounded by the happy sounds of other animals chatting and playing, he knew, in time, his heart would heal.

When he emerged from the water, he felt fresh and new. As he dried off, shaking the water from his coat before lying in the sun, he and Little Bean giggled together on the grassy banks while they watched Ankel preen in the mirrorlike water. It was nearly noon by the time Dilah reluctantly followed Ankel and Little Bean to the registration area beside the stage, feeling jittery and nervous all over again.

An otter stood by the stage greeting contestants. "Quick, quick—it's nearly time for the first round!" he said. "Birds who cluck, caw, and fly, line up here." He pointed to one side of the stage. "Animals who jump, hop, and walk, line up over there!" Dilah found himself standing in a long line of animals that included minks, weasels, rabbits, deer, and black bears, each one beautiful in their own way. He gulped. The competition was fierce! There were fewer entrants in the bird group. He spotted a myriad of brightly plumed birds whose species he couldn't name, alongside pheasants, chickens, and hazel grouses impatiently waiting in line, *cluck-cluck-cluck*ing. The idea of the beauty contest, pitting species against species, was baffling to Dilah—how was anyone supposed to judge?

"Come on!" said Ankel, urging Dilah forward. "I've registered our names. Let's get in line!"

A large animal audience had gathered to watch the primary round of the pageant, trying to guess which animals might make the top four. Two sables scurried through the crowd, encouraging everyone to place bets on this year's winner.

Finally, it was Dilah's turn to stand before the three judges: a rabbit, a lynx, and an elk. His stomach clenched uncomfortably, and he felt he might actually be sick. He hurried onstage, eager to put an end to his misery. The judges peered at him in obvious curiosity and admiration.

"Wow, I love his color!" the middle-aged female rabbit gushed, nodding approvingly. "And look how fluffy his coat is!"

"Are you from the Arctic?" asked the elderly yellow lynx hoarsely. He sized Dilah up with a careful, critical look in his eyes, stroking his fur and tugging on his tail. He didn't wait for Dilah to reply before adding, "Of course you are. Marvelous, so unusual."

Dilah was already fuming. He hated being looked up and down like this and spoken of as if he weren't standing right there. Didn't they know he wasn't an object? He had thoughts and feelings too! He caught Little Bean's eye at the front of the crowd, and the rabbit nodded encouragingly. Dilah's anger flooded out of him, and he breathed deeply, remembering his purpose: Win the contest, win the map. Continue on his quest to transform into a human.

The elk judge cleared his throat. "I'd like to ask something unrelated to the competition. They say at the North Pole, you can see the most wonderful lights in the sky . . . What is that like?"

"They're called the aurora borealis, or northern lights," Dilah stiffly replied, feeling patronized. "They're very pretty."

"Lastly, make a turn—like that, great. That should do it," the lynx said.

Dilah leapt from the stage gratefully, joining Little Bean in the crowd—but he didn't stray very far, as Ankel was next. The judges stared at Ankel's shiny little head and frowned. *"Another* weasel?" the elk muttered. The assessment was over rather quickly. Ankel seemed to know that the result wasn't good, walking over to Dilah and Little Bean with his head hanging low.

"Don't be sad. They don't understand how to appreciate your beauty," Little Bean said, patting Ankel's shoulders as the next contestant was assessed. "Besides, there were quite a lot of weasels. It was difficult for you to stand out."

Ankel nodded, feeling a little better.

"Hmph! Get out of the way!" A colorful green peacock leapt from the birds' side of the stage and snarled at the animal blocking his tail. He strutted over to a tree marked as the contestants' resting area, finding the perfect patch of shade as he waited haughtily. Dilah stared at the bird. Despite his bad attitude, surely he was the most beautiful creature in the world: enchanting eyes, a gorgeous crown, a long and slender neck, fluorescent feathers all over, and a long, elegant tail. What chance did Dilah have against such an animal?

After what felt like a never-ending wait, the rabbit judge rushed over to the resting area. "The primaries have finished. After much discussion among the judges, I am happy to announce the four finalists." All of the animals perked up their ears and gazed expectantly at the rabbit. "They are as follows: from the bird group, the hazel grouse Sherry and the peacock Blaine; from the beast group, the sable Indigo and the Arctic fox Dilah."

Dilah was shocked to hear his own name, two very different feelings twisting inside his stomach. He was happy, of course, because the map of the enchanted forest was nearly in reach. But . . . he really didn't relish the thought of standing on the stage again and being "appreciated" by more animals.

"Excellent! I knew our tactic would pay off!" Ankel said, seemingly over his earlier disappointment. Dilah suspected he was a little relieved not to have to go through more judging too.

———◇———

Once again, Bing climbed onstage and cleared his throat to gain the crowd's attention. "Ladies and gentlemen, welcome to the final round of the third Beauty Pageant of the Primeval Forest!

"I'd like to invite our four finalists to the stage. First up, the winner of our last beauty pageant, from the 'cluck and caw' group, may I present to you Miss Sherry, a hazel grouse!" A glossy-feathered hazel grouse strolled onto the stage and bowed to the audience, who cheered for her enthusiastically.

"Next up, also from the 'cluck and caw' group, may I present to you Mr. Blaine, a peacock!" The arrogant peacock gracefully sashayed onto the stage. The audience erupted into applause, but there were also several boos and hisses.

"And now, may I present to you, from the 'jump and hop' group, Mr. Indigo, a rare sable!" A handsome sable nervously stepped up, tripped on the edge of the stage, and fell to the floor with a thud. He scrambled to his feet and shyly peered at the audience, which made them roar with laughter.

Bing signaled for them all to quiet down. "My dear audience, this get-together of ours isn't merely limited to the creatures of this particular forest. It's so world-renowned that an extraordinary animal has traveled all the way from the Arctic to join us, the first time this has happened in my ten years as host."

If he hadn't been so nervous, Dilah would have rolled his eyes. He'd hardly traveled all this way for the get-together, and especially not for a beauty pageant!

"Last, but not least, from the 'jump and hop' group, I'd like to give a special welcome to Mr. Dilah, an Arctic fox!"

The audience clapped and cheered and whistled as Dilah hesitantly stepped up to the stage, where Bing motioned for him to stand at the front with the other three contestants. Gazing out over the enormous crowd, he thought he was going to pass out—but then he caught sight of Ankel and Little Bean, cheering for him enthusiastically. Ankel caught his eye and motioned for Dilah to breathe deeply—so he did, three times, eventually feeling the *thud-thud* of his heart slow down.

"Wonderful, now all four of our finalists are here onstage. Let me explain how the judging works. Our jury is composed of six professional judges from the 'cluck and caw' and 'jump and hop' groups. Each one is an authority in the beauty realm, and each has a sharp set of eyes and strict aesthetic standards—there's no need to question their taste. The six judges will rate the color, fur or feathers, physique, movement, disposition, and popularity of each contestant on a scale of one to ten. The total combined score will be the final score for each contestant, and the winner will be the one with the highest score. Each contestant is required to walk once around the stage. As they walk, they are encouraged to showcase various beautiful movements to win the judges' favor and the audience's support. OK, let's get this show on the road. The first contestant is . . . Sherry!"

Bing stood in the center of the stage, and the speckle-tailed hazel grouse circled around him, then pranced to the edge of the stage like a pro. She had vibrantly colored feathers and a flowerlike tail and—even more importantly, thought Dilah—loads of confidence. She flaunted her talent for dancing, sashaying with elegant steps, her slender neck nimbly swaying.

Next up was the sable, who tottered onto the stage looking a little like Dilah felt. He was clearly nervous, but his rare fur—a rich black that almost shone purple—was extremely eye-catching.

He was followed by the peacock, who sauntered to the middle of the stage and then, with a drumroll-like rustle, stretched out his tail toward the judges. The crowd gasped. His tail was a resplendent fan, its markings like countless eyes glowing sapphire and green in the sun.

Finally, it was Dilah's turn. He took a deep breath and shakily walked out in front of the others. The gazes of the six judges turned his whole body stiff with nerves.

"Walk in a straight line . . . a straight line . . ." Dilah muttered to himself, robotically alternating his limbs. Despite the applause, he was sure he resembled an over-sized cub learning to walk for the first time. He sighed in relief as he completed his circuit and stood beside the other three finalists, his body sagging in disappointment. Surely he'd messed everything up!

A long, muttering interlude started. The crowd and the judges discussed the four contestants, speculating who would, and should, be the winner.

"All right, dear audience, after watching those delight-ful performances, do you have a clear favorite? To be honest, I do, but I can't yet say." Bing winked playfully at the crowd. "All right, then, without any further ado, let's hear the judges' scores. We'll start with Sherry!" The judges held up little wooden slates with numbers carved into their surface as Bing read out each category.

"Color: nine points! Feathers: eight! Physique: eight! Movement: ten! Disposition: seven! Popularity: ten! A total of fifty-two points!" Bing exclaimed.

"And now, let's move on to our next contestant, Indigo!

Color: nine! Fur: ten! Physique: seven! Movement: seven! Disposition: seven! Popularity: eight! Forty-eight points total!" Bing declared.

"Next up, the scores for our third contestant, Blaine! Color: ten! Feathers: ten! Physique: ten! Movement: nine! Disposition: nine! Popularity: eight! . . . Oh my! A total of fifty-six points, a near perfect score! We have a clear leader!" Bing proclaimed.

"And now, for our final contestant, Dilah! Color: ten! Fur: ten! Physique: ten! Movement: eight! Disposition: eight! Popularity: ten! A total of . . . fifty-six points!" Bing bellowed. "Whoa! We have a tie. Two equally beautiful animals! But there's only one map, and according to the rules, Dilah and Blaine must face off in a tiebreak round."

"What?! I received the same score as this . . . *ordinary* fox?" Blaine blurted out, visibly annoyed.

"Dilah is no ordinary fox. He's—" Bing tried to explain.

"He's *plain*! What kind of beauty standards are you using? Do you have any taste?!" Blaine snapped at the judges. "I'll have you know, I'm a distant relative of the phoenix, one of the ancient sacred animals!" Before the sound of his voice had even died down, *thwack*—a pine cone hit him in the face.

"Who did that? Who had the *gall* to do that?" Blaine fumed, looking all around and ruffling his feathers angrily. A flying squirrel snickered as he climbed a tree trunk, his large, bushy tail dangling, his small paw clutching another pine cone.

"Listen, Blaine," Bing said soothingly, "based on the scores, you two do need to have another round. The rules don't allow for a tie for the winner."

"It's beneath me to compete against this fox in the first place, let alone have a tiebreaker. I'm the king of the birds!" Blaine ranted.

"Arrogant twerp!" someone in the crowd cawed.

"Is he even a wild animal?" growled a disgruntled wolf.

"Yeah, he looks like he escaped from a peacock farm!" chirped a little bird.

"Disqualify him!" several others raged.

The crowd fired off taunt after taunt. Blaine was obviously flustered—the judges too. Dilah stood silently, unsure whether he should intervene.

At last, Blaine let out an eerie scream that silenced the crowd. "Hmph!" he exclaimed. "What's the point of winning a prize in a place with such low standards, anyway? I quit!" He turned around, leapt from the stage, and flew away, leaving behind a colorful gleam.

Dilah blinked as his only remaining competitor disappeared into the distance. Did this mean . . .

Bing cleared his throat. "Now that Blaine has forfeited . . . well, it's my honor to declare Arctic fox Dilah as the winner of the third Beauty Pageant of the Primeval Forest!"

The crowd went wild, the animals all chanting Dilah's name in unison. Dilah blinked. Had he really just . . . won the map? He found Ankel and Little Bean in the crowd—both were jumping up and down and cheering.

"All I have to say is that this is truly a well-deserved achievement," continued Bing. "Please welcome the chair of the jury—a master of modern aesthetics—Mr. Birkin, to present the prize to our winner, Dilah!"

The elderly yellow lynx slowly made his way to the stage, clutching a thick sheaf of sheepskin.

Dilah barely listened as Birkin croaked his speech through the loudspeaker. At last, solemnly, he turned to Dilah and handed him the sheaf, which Dilah held carefully in his mouth. The crowd sighed with envy.

"Is there anything you'd like to say?" Bing kindly asked Dilah.

Dilah placed the map carefully at his feet. "Er—I don't think so." Dilah was at a loss for words.

"C'mon, say a little something!"

Everyone was watching expectantly . . . so Dilah stepped up to the loudspeaker. "Um, to be honest, I'm very surprised to have won the pageant. This brings me one step closer to my dream. I'd like to thank the judges for their generous appraisal, as well as my friends: Ankel, Little Bean, and . . . Emily . . . although she's not here right now . . ." Dilah cleared his throat as he felt it tighten with emotion. "Anyway, thank you, all. It really means a lot."

———◇———

There were paw shakes and congratulations as Dilah was ushered from judge to judge, and dusk had fallen as he finally stepped off the stage, the sun turning the clouds into streaks of warm orange red. Several migratory birds soared through the air, emitting drawn-out low cries that sent shivers down Dilah's spine.

The crowd was scattering, the animals in the volcanic basin gradually returning to wherever they were sleeping for the night. Ankel and Little Bean bounced around Dilah excitedly as he carried the map to them.

"You did it! You did it!" Ankel said, clapping his little hands together.

Little Bean hopped in delight. "I knew you'd win," he said, a little pride in his voice.

Dilah noticed Bing exiting the stage from the other side. The old goat had been the one to announce the map as the prize, and he'd insisted it was "tried and tested." Had he himself ventured to the enchanted forest? "Wait a second," Dilah said to his friends, shoving the map into Ankel's hands. "Mr. Bing . . . excuse me," Dilah called. The goat turned.

"Ah, Dilah—our champion! I have to admit, I'm disappointed you won't be staying to celebrate your victory tomorrow. Are you sure I can't persuade you?"

Bing had invited Dilah to a great feast tomorrow at noon, but Dilah had declined; it was high time they continued on their quest, now that they had the map. "I'm sorry," Dilah said, "we have to continue our journey. But I was wondering . . . Have you heard of the spring of reincarnation in the enchanted forest?"

"Spring of reincarnation?" The goat looked thoughtful. "I only know of the enchanted spring, hidden deep in the forest. Perhaps it's the same thing?" Bing asked, eyeing Dilah curiously.

"Maybe." Dilah cocked his ears. "What do animals say about it?"

"Some say it has marvelous healing properties . . . Others say powers of transformation." The goat's red-rimmed eyes gleamed with canny intelligence. "Why do you ask?"

Dilah decided to play ignorant—better not to spread word about their quest with enemies at large. "Oh, I heard some animals talking about the spring. They were wondering if the map would show its location."

"I see," said Bing. Dilah had the impression he wasn't

fooled, but the old goat didn't press the point. "Well, in any case, if you're heading straight for the enchanted forest, you'll want to go that way." The goat pointed his gnarled horns over one of the extinct volcanoes.

Dilah nodded gratefully. "Well then, Mr. Bing, I guess this is goodbye. May you live a long and healthy life!"

"And you, young fox. Good luck."

Dilah joined Ankel and Little Bean, who was clutching the map tightly between his forelegs. "Come on," said Dilah, "this way."

They left at once, ascending the shallow slope of the volcano until they had a magnificent view of the forest they'd left behind. Dilah glanced back, reflecting on all that had happened there. Emily's smile floated above the forest, her voice echoing in his ears.

"Goodbye," Dilah whispered, then hurried to join his friends.

CHAPTER 4

The Mist

The moon peeked out from the clouds, casting bright light onto the vast grassland on the other side of the volcano. Dilah stopped and opened up the map. It was a square piece of thick sheepskin with a string of red text written on the upper left corner. Dilah recognized the language as Classical Animalese—an ancient animal script that very few animals now living could read. Luckily, Dilah knew at least one of them . . .

"'Land of Abundance,'" read Ankel. His grandfather

had taught him the language, along with many other things, when he was very small.

Dilah glanced at him. "What do you think? Is it real?"

"The map seems very old, and the Classical Animalese is written correctly and coherently. I don't think it's a forgery," Ankel replied.

"So . . . can you see the enchanted forest?" Little Bean piped up.

"Heaven Pool Ridge, Wood Ridge . . ." Ankel studied the map, mumbling.

"It's here, the enchanted forest!" Ankel shouted, pointing to a blank spot on the map surrounded by four mountains. The nearby terrain was clearly marked, but there was nothing there, other than the words "Enchanted Forest" written in faded script. "Hmm, let's see . . . It's near Drum Mountain, Greenwood Peak, Jessup Mountain . . ."

Little Bean hopped with excitement. "I can't wait to see where Lord Lund's ancestors are from!" Dilah remembered the gentle, giant rabbit who had a fondness for dozing off. He was the one who'd first told them about the enchanted forest.

"But why is the enchanted forest empty?" Ankel was perplexed. "It's like they forgot to draw it!"

Dilah shivered with excitement. "I guess we'll find out once we're there."

"I bet there're all sorts of exotic plants!" Little Bean clasped his paws.

"Can you see where we are on the map?" Dilah asked Ankel. "How far do we have to go?"

The weasel scratched his chin as he scanned the old hide. It felt like a long time before he finally pointed at a circle of volcanoes at the very top of the map, on the opposite side of the forest. "A long, long way," he said.

———◇———

The weeks and miles whizzed by in the blink of an eye as Dilah, Ankel, and Little Bean traveled south. Despite the relentlessly terrible weather, Dilah felt strengthened by renewed purpose and direction. Food was plentiful and humans few and far between. Eventually, they reached a long mountain chain—so long that, from afar, it resembled a winding green snake, with clouds and mist curling up in layers of bright and dark green. At the foot of the mountains, they met a gazelle chewing on the long grass.

"Hello. Do you happen to know how to get to the Land of Abundance?" Ankel asked, naming the area on the map in which the enchanted forest was hidden.

"Why, you're in it!" the gazelle replied.

Smiles spread across the faces of the three friends. After a long journey, they were finally close.

"Thank you!" Ankel said to the gazelle. "And do you happen to know Heaven Pool Ridge and Wood Ridge?"

"I've just come from that way. They're on the west side of the mountain, a few hills over." The gazelle gestured with his nose.

"Got it! Thank you!" Dilah said.

Dilah led Ankel and Little Bean through the hills. The terrain was lush and green, with bamboo groves swaying in the breeze. Dazzling streams flowed through the hills, like ribbons of light guiding their path.

—◇—

A few days later, they came upon a round lake. From the high slopes where they stood, it looked like a sapphire that had fallen from the sky, sparkling blue and crystal clear all at once. They could even clearly make out the sunken deadwood at the bottom.

"Um, let me see . . . I think this is Heaven Pool Ridge . . ." Ankel stood atop the mountain and peered into the distance, consulting the map. "That should be Drum Mountain over there!"

They descended to the lake, where a troop of golden monkeys were scampering around the water's edge, shooting up and down the trees mischievously. Dilah called to them, asking if they were heading the right way for Drum Mountain.

"You sure are!" one shouted back. "And how about this for a drumming?" With that, the monkeys cackled as they pelted the friends with volleys of rotten nuts.

"Not everything's heavenly here after all!" joked Ankel as the three hurried on their way.

———◇———

Another two days' walking brought them to the base of Drum Mountain, and they started to climb. At the top, they opened the map again, barely able to contain their excitement. Strangely, there was a large area below them enveloped in a peculiar dense mist. Dilah peered at the blank spot on the map, his heart pattering.

"The thick mist below us," he said, "it's hiding the enchanted forest. We're nearly there!"

"That's the enchanted forest?" Little Bean said. "But why can't we even see any treetops?"

"Plus, it's noon—there shouldn't be so much mist . . ." Ankel said, scratching his head.

"Let's go check it out," Dilah said, unperturbed.

The three friends carefully made their way down the mountain, then plunged into the shifting sea of dense mist. The mist blocked the sun so completely that only the faintest rays of light streamed through. All they could make out was dull whiteness. Dilah took a few steps forward—then something snapped under his paw. When he realized what it was, he stumbled backward, nearly knocking Little Bean over.

The ground was littered with incomplete animal skeletons.

"What happened here?" Ankel asked, horror creeping into his voice.

Suddenly, Dilah felt more frightened than excited. How had these animals died? How many secrets were hidden behind the thick mist? Was this an enchanted forest . . . or a trap? Fear of the unknown began to erode his courage.

"We need to stay close together," Dilah cautioned. He heard a rustling behind him. He looked all around, but there was nothing there but the suffocating fog.

"At least now we know why the enchanted forest is blank on the map," Ankel grumbled.

They passed a group of pine trees, their shadows looming in the faint sunlight.

"Look at this!" Ankel had found something and held it out in his paw.

Dilah sniffed at the round, shiny object. It had a dial on the front under a glass covering. "What is it?" he asked.

"A compass—one of the greatest inventions of ancient times. Humans use it to navigate."

"Humans must've been here!" Dilah realized. They could clearly see the needle in the compass wiggling back and forth, never settling on one direction. Little Bean hopped over to see for himself.

"What's wrong with it?" Little Bean asked. "Or is it supposed to be doing that?"

"No . . . it's supposed to point north. Hmm . . . Maybe something's disturbed it . . ." Ankel studied the object carefully, frowning.

"Let's just leave it. It's obviously broken," Dilah said. "We should carry on, try to find the enchanted forest before nightfall."

They headed deeper into the mist, but it appeared that all it was hiding was a silent and lifeless pine forest, filled with bare bones and the stench of death.

They'd been walking for an hour when, once again, they came upon a compass beneath a tree.

"Another one?" Little Bean asked, flustered.

Dilah sniffed it, shook his head. "It's the same one," he said, his despair growing.

"In other words, we just went in a circle," Ankel groaned.

A twig snapped nearby—but though the three friends spun to face whoever or whatever was watching, nothing emerged from the mist.

Dilah let out a deep sigh. "OK, let's try again. This time, we'll go in a different direction."

The three friends headed off to their right. Dilah paid particular attention to trying not to veer off course. But after walking for a while, the worst thing happened: They came upon the compass yet again!

"No way!" Ankel said, exasperated, as he recognized the device.

"I think we're officially lost," said Little Bean.

A tiny mouse scurried out of the empty eye socket of what looked like a bear skull and let out a bloodcurdling scream before disappearing into the mist.

"I don't like this one bit. Let's go back to Drum Mountain," Dilah said calmly. "Hopefully, we can get our bearings there."

They headed back out of the forest. But Dilah was sure he could hear something—something big—lumbering through the trees a short distance away. A moment later, Dilah whispered to Ankel and Little Bean, "We're being followed—shh—don't let on that we know."

"Let's go faster," Ankel whispered back uneasily.

They picked up their pace, but whatever was following them adjusted its pace too, following so closely that it could no longer cover up the thud of its heavy footsteps. They heard the rustle of dead leaves being trampled.

This was no small animal.

Sensing that the beast was gaining, Dilah suggested they run the other way.

They took off, bolting as fast as they could, and the footsteps grew fainter and fainter. They were sure they'd shaken it off until they came upon a gigantic figure blocking their path.

"Trying to lose me?" a deep voice rumbled.

A giant panda stood in the mist, gripping a tree. He was young, big, and strong, his fur matted and disheveled. He had a round white belly, thick black limbs, and a hat perched on his head—a *hat*?! It was the kind of hat that humans wore to guard against the rain, woven from bamboo. The brim of the hat covered his eyes mysteriously.

"Who are you? Why are you following us?" Dilah demanded, standing protectively in front of Ankel and Little Bean.

"Are you looking for the enchanted forest?" the panda asked.

Ankel immediately hid the map behind his back.

"Don't be afraid. I'm not here to steal your map. I already know what it looks like."

"Then why are you following us?" Dilah asked, narrowing his eyes.

"I've got a map but still can't find the forest. I'm hoping I can join you on your journey."

Dilah relaxed a little, relieved the panda didn't appear to mean them any immediate harm. "Why do you want to go to the enchanted forest?"

"I want to go to the legendary spring of reincarnation. I—" The panda broke off, as if he'd decided against saying whatever he was about to say.

"Spring of reincarnation?" Dilah asking, exchanging looks with Ankel and Little Bean. Bing and others had referred to the "enchanted spring," but the panda was the first to call it the "spring of reincarnation" since Lord Lund had told them about it. "How do you know about that?"

"From a black bear. I also got the map from him. He told me that the enchanted forest was near Drum Mountain, but he died before he could tell me exactly how to get there," the panda explained, adjusting the hat on his head to better cover his eyes.

"Died?" Ankel asked, frightened.

"Oh, maybe I hit him too hard," the panda said coldly. "How was I supposed to know he was so weak?"

Dilah didn't think the panda was bluffing. He sounded much too confident. But Dilah was chilled by his emotionless tone.

The panda continued. "I've been searching this mist for weeks. I'll never find the forest on my own. I decided to wait for other animals to show up, and follow them."

"If you've been following us," said Dilah, "you must've seen us going around in circles. We've been no more successful than you in finding the forest."

"You've only been trying for a few hours. I believe you can do it," the panda said, slightly menacingly. "Let's make a deal. You take me with you to the enchanted forest, and I'll protect you along the way."

"Protect us from what?"

The panda met Dilah's eyes. "You don't want to know, little fox. You've been lucky so far."

Dilah gulped. "But what if we can't find it?"

"Then you should know that I struggle to control my temper," the panda said, quietly and unfeelingly. "I hope you'll seriously consider my request. It won't do you any harm to take me with you."

"I can only promise to—" Dilah began.

"It's a deal!" the panda cut in.

Dilah had little choice. "Fine. But you must promise not to hurt my friends."

"Of course . . . as long as you lead me to the enchanted forest," the panda replied. "And since we're traveling together, we should introduce ourselves. I'm Tyrone."

Dilah, Ankel, and Little Bean introduced themselves uneasily.

"We were planning on spending the night outside the mist and returning tomorrow," Ankel said.

The panda laughed humorlessly. "That's not going to happen. Once you enter the fog, there's no way out. What do you think all these skeletons are, hmm?" He gestured at the detritus of animal remains on the ground. "They got lost searching for the forest or trying to escape from the mist and simply wasted away . . . or were picked off by some of the dangers I mentioned."

Little Bean, Ankel, and Dilah exchanged worried glances. "OK," said Dilah. "Let's carry on searching."

They set off back into the fog, choosing what they were

certain was a different direction. Night was falling, and as they passed by pine after pine, they once again came upon the compass beneath the tree.

"We're trapped," Ankel said with dread.

Little Bean shivered. "We're going to end up just like these bones, lost and starved to death."

"Unless I kill you first," the panda growled.

"Calm down," Dilah said. "Let's think this through. Whatever direction we choose, we keep coming back to the compass." Dilah frowned down at the human implement. "It must be some kind of magic."

"Compass . . . compass . . ." Ankel was deep in thought, nibbling on his claws. Then he sat up straight. "Don't we have an even better 'compass'?" His beady black eyes gleamed.

"Do you mean . . . ?" Dilah realized what he was implying and gasped. Little Bean and Ankel clapped.

Tyrone frowned. "What are you on about?"

The others ignored him. "Will it work with such faint moonlight?" Ankel pursed his lips.

"Let's give it a try and find out!" Dilah was hopeful.

"What're you talking about?" the big panda asked.

"Just wait, you'll see," Little Bean said, smiling. "But we can't do anything until nighttime."

The sun was setting, the sky growing darker and darker, the mist turning pink and then deepest red. They didn't have to wait long after that. Soon, the fog turned silver as the moon rose in the night sky.

Dilah removed the parcel from around his neck and opened it beneath the pale, filtered moonlight. The moonstone lay motionless in the chilly darkness. The three friends and the panda stared at it expectantly.

"Is something supposed to happen?" said Tyrone grumpily.

Dilah was about to give up when the small golden crescent in the center of the stone emitted a faint, flickering glow.

"Whoa . . ." said the panda.

The moon started spinning feebly until at last it stopped, a beam of quivering light pointing straight through the fog. Unlike the compass arrow, it was steady and true.

"Success!" Dilah cried excitedly.

CHAPTER 5

The Enchanted Forest

Dilah and his friends headed through the darkness, following the moonstone's beam to keep from walking in circles. Even so, the route felt like a maze—they zigzagged back and forth, and at another point felt as if they were walking around in a big spiral. But they kept faith in the moonstone, and gradually the mist began to lift, the temperature warmed, the air grew fresher, and more and more vegetation sprang up until the sparse pine trees gave way to lush and thick foliage. They looked around in surprise. All of a sudden, they were now in what looked to be . . .

"The enchanted forest!" said Tyrone. "At last!"

Dilah had never seen anything quite like it. The grass and trees in the warm, humid forest were taller than anywhere else he'd been on his long journey. Thick green moss blanketed nearly every trunk, and tall ferns fanned out beneath the giant oaks, banyans, and pines. Countless thick vines were hanging from their boughs, roots raised and tangled on the ground.

The three friends shivered, their bodies instinctively sensing a formidable force oozing from the forest. It felt as though some sort of magic had dissolved in the air, brimming with endless mystery—as if the forest was an ancient creature containing a bellyful of stories and secrets.

"Let's rest awhile," Dilah suggested softly. "We can carry on in the morning. The main thing is, we're here now."

———◇———

The following morning, the birds gently roused them from their dreams with sweet, drawn-out songs. Warm sunlight cascaded down like a waterfall, and the leaves glistened with beads of dew. While the world beyond the mist had been shifting into winter, here it was spring, with birds chirping and flowers blooming.

Roused from their leafy bed, the three friends and the panda passed by towering trees entwined with maple vines as they started to explore, searching for the mythical spring. As far as the eye could see, the ground overflowed with strange flowers and plants, the majority of which

even Little Bean couldn't name. The rabbit excitedly hopped from one plant to the next, wishing he could stop to study their effects. Dilah watched happily as he bounded through the flowers and grass, smelling the large pink flowers; stroking a bunch of blueberries that exuded sweet, pleasant aromas; and shaking a gigantic red-and-white-spotted mushroom until a giant caterpillar crawled out of the grass and gave him such a fright he fell on his backside.

Once Dilah and Ankel were done laughing—Tyrone sat in stony silence, refusing to join in—Dilah said, "Come on, let's carry on exploring. We should pick up the pace."

They'd walked for a couple of miles more when Dilah spotted a flash of orange in the grass. Before he could make out what it was, a deafening roar rang out. He spun toward it, and his heart jumped up to his throat. A tiger leapt through the air at Little Bean, baring his teeth and claws!

"Watch out!" Dilah cried.

The tiger struck Little Bean on the back, and the rabbit fell to the ground with a thud.

The tiger opened his mouth and was about to sink his teeth into the rabbit when Tyrone lunged forward, protecting Little Bean with his arm. The tiger bit down hard. Blood spattered from the wound, but, roaring, the giant panda swung his injured arm around the tiger's neck and yanked him away from Little Bean. The tiger tried to dig into the forest floor, but his claws only scraped across the ground as Tyrone dragged him away. The panda's strength was incredible.

The tiger cowered as Tyrone released him, but then glared at the panda with a murderous look of surprise.

Tyrone widened his stance, bracing himself for the tiger's attack. Dilah thought the pair appeared equally matched: The tiger and the panda were a similar size, the tiger's body lean and strong to match Tyrone's muscular bulk. The panda stared into the tiger's eyes and circled him slowly, unbothered by the open wound on his arm.

Then the tiger pounced. Tyrone lurched aside, swinging his fleshy paw. The tiger dodged the blow, stood up on his hind legs, and lunged at Tyrone's neck, fierce teeth bared. Tyrone ducked out of the way, but the tiger chomped down on his bamboo hat, smashing the bamboo strips with a *snap*. The tiger tore the battered hat off the panda's head. At last, the panda's face was revealed: He had a pair of small furry ears, a round black nose, and tiny, bright black eyes embedded in two black circles of fur.

Dilah had a hard time accepting that a fierce beast that could go head to head with a tiger could have such a sweet and charming face.

At the sight of his smashed bamboo hat, the panda roared with fury and charged at the tiger. *Thud*—both animals fell to the ground, but the nimbler tiger quickly righted himself from under the panda's bulk. *Why is Tyrone so angry about a silly hat?* Dilah wondered. *Does he not want others to see his face?*

As the panda tried to rise to his feet, the tiger flicked his tail against Tyrone's back heel. He lost his balance and fell down again with a crash. The tiger pounced, clamping Tyrone's broad shoulders to the ground with his paws, but the panda rolled over, pulled the tiger to the ground, and punched him once, hard, in the jaw.

Suddenly, Dilah heard the clip-clop of galloping heels

and turned toward the noise. A huge creature—a deer of some kind, thought Dilah—flew out of the violet bushes and ran toward the panda and tiger. The deer forcefully separated the two animals with a flick of his hoof. The two fighters stared up at the large animal, the morning light shining down like a spotlight.

The unusually tall, dark-furred deer emerged from the halo of light. He had deep-set eyes, and his huge horns were perched high on his head. Dilah thought the white spots dotting his back were as lovely as stars.

"This is not a place for fighting. Please cease—or leave at once," the deer politely instructed, his voice refined and pleasant.

"You rascal . . . You only meet your match once in a blue moon," Tyrone said to the tiger, shaking the blood from his arm as he stepped away from his opponent.

"It's admirable to see a panda with such skill," the tiger said, ducking into the tall grass and slinking off, watched by the tall deer.

"Thank you!" Little Bean said to Tyrone. "You saved my life."

"No need to thank me. I wouldn't have saved you if I hadn't promised to protect you all," the panda coolly replied. He picked up his chewed hat and studied it with a pained gaze, a trace of warmth in his eyes—the first time Dilah had seen Tyrone express any kind of emotion.

"Tyrone, we need to stop the bleeding on your arm," Little Bean said gently. "Come with me."

Tyrone didn't budge.

"If you don't let me treat it, your wound might get infected!"

Putting on his battered hat, Tyrone reluctantly walked over to the rabbit, who started to gather a bundle of plants and flowers for his treatment.

"Thank you for intervening," said Dilah to the deer. "If you don't mind me saying, you seem bigger than most deer I've seen." Little Bean had set to work nearby, chewing a bunch of thick leaves for a poultice.

"Oh, that's because of the spring. All plants and animals here are larger than they are in the world outside," the deer explained.

"The spring?" Ankel's ears twitched in curiosity.

"Do you mean the spring of reincarnation?" Dilah asked cautiously.

"Aha, so you came in search of that." The deer's voice turned serious. "You want to become human."

"Yes. We've traveled thousands of miles on our quest . . . Please will you help us find the spring?" Dilah asked.

But the deer stomped his hoof angrily. "What's so great about humans? They've polluted much of the outside world, destroying forests, rivers, and the atmosphere; mining minerals, trees, and energy to the point of exhaustion; driving once-brilliant animals to extinction. They've scarred and battered the entire earth. Humans don't value their own lives. They desecrate the gift of nature with crime, murder, and war. There's no end to their desire to control everything . . ."

"Yes . . ." Dilah replied softly, "there are people who pollute the environment . . . but there are also people who protect it. There are people who waste resources, but also people who save resources, people who kill wild animals, but people who protect them . . ."

"That's just a small fraction, not everyone—"

But Dilah interrupted. "I will be one of those humans—the ones who protect the environment, animals, and resources. If I'm human, I'll have more power to do good in the world. And so will all my friends. That's why I'm looking for the spring of reincarnation!"

Apparently moved by Dilah's words, the deer blinked his long eyelashes and sighed. "I understand. Come with me. If you're all ready?"

Little Bean had finished wrapping Tyrone's injured arm in a large leaf, his poultice stopping an infection from forming beneath. So the deer gracefully led the way, Dilah, Ankel, Little Bean, and Tyrone following behind.

"My name is Fario," said the deer as they walked. "I'm one of the guardians of the forest. My job is to help those animals who venture here and to keep the peace among all our residents."

"Have you heard of the giant rabbit clan?" Ankel asked with interest.

"Of course! They used to live in the enchanted forest, but unfortunately, they've gone extinct. They moved out of the forest a long time ago."

"They didn't go extinct. The chief of our tribe is a giant rabbit!" Little Bean rushed to explain.

The deer wanted to know more, and he and the rabbit proceeded to talk as they continued on through the forest.

Sunlight shone through the branches, shadows flickering. The trees grew larger and larger the deeper they traveled. Their luxuriant branches and leaves were like green clouds blocking the sun. A strange feeling came over Dilah—it felt to him that they were secretly being watched. The trees rustled, as if whispering in their ears.

"Those are tree sprites," Fario said as he noticed Dilah's curious glances up at the trees. "They're sunbathing. Don't disturb them."

After a while, the forest opened into a clearing, revealing a spotless sky above as blue as the moonstone.

"This is as far as I'm able to take you," Fario said, drawing to a halt. "I have another job to which I must attend. From here on out, the rest is up to you." He nodded toward the far side of the clearing. "There's a stream through there. Follow it down to a lake, round the lake, and find a waterfall. That's where you'll discover what you're looking for." And with that, Fario left them, fleet-footed, disappearing into the trees.

Dilah, Ankel, Little Bean, and Tyrone continued across the clearing, navigating their way around thick tree roots.

On the far side, they heard a trickling sound.

"Come on," said Dilah, "that must be the stream!" He bounded ahead, excited their journey was finally drawing to its close.

Sure enough, a winding stream coursed through the ancient oaks. The bottom of the stream was paved with round pebbles. The water was crystal clear in the sun, diamonds of water tumbling in the spray. The friends gathered around and gratefully drank from it. A faint medicinal scent filled their noses and mouths.

"Like licorice and bitter almonds," Little Bean said.

After he finished drinking, Tyrone glanced down at the bound wound on his arm, frowning. To Little Bean's horror, he lifted away the carefully fastened bandage—only to find the injury had completely healed!

"Wow!" said Little Bean, hopping over in disbelief to inspect Tyrone's arm. "How is that possible?"

"It must be the water!" said Dilah, splashing about happily. "I already feel like I have more energy than ever before."

"Me too." Ankel smiled, his small round head gleaming with stream water.

Once they'd drunk their fill, the four friends walked along the stream as the deer had directed. They'd been traveling all day, and the sun was starting to set. After a while, they approached a dense grove of bushes. Pushing through, they came upon a tranquil lake, the water as pitch-black as ink. Two huge white swans floated serenely in the middle of the lake, every now and then poking their curved necks under their wings to preen their feathers.

As night fell, stars twinkled in a magnificent silver river across the evening sky. The four animals didn't feel tired at all. They walked on, around the narrow black lake in the moonlight. As they passed a grassy area to their right, countless fireflies rose up, soaring in the air, glimmering like yellow stars. Dilah, Ankel, Tyrone, and Little Bean had never seen such a breathtaking sight. In high spirits, the three old friends chased one another and play fought among the sea of flickering stars while Tyrone watched, his face stony. Dilah couldn't help but wonder if, deep down, the stoic panda wished he could join in.

At last, the friends tired one another out and prepared to sleep beneath the trees at the lake's edge. Ankel was snoring within minutes.

After a time, Tyrone walked to the edge of the lake alone and sat in the dark, leaning against a thick tree trunk, caressing the broken bamboo hat and staring dreamily into the distance. Tyrone's silhouette seemed lonely and weathered. Dilah was sleepily wondering whether to approach the panda when he saw Little Bean hop over to the great bear.

"Are you all right?" asked Little Bean, a sympathetic expression in his brown eyes.

Tyrone glanced up, then quickly looked away, pretending that he hadn't heard. An owl hooted in the distance.

"Tyrone . . . are you all right?" Little Bean repeated, peering with concern.

"I'm . . . How come you're still awake?" Tyrone snapped.

"I saw you hadn't gone to bed. I figured you must have something on your mind."

"It's none of your business!" Tyrone turned away again, closed his eyes, and pretended to sleep, then sneakily opened one eye to see whether Little Bean had gone away.

Little Bean was still standing there, staring down at his feet. "I don't know what happened to you. Whatever it was, I'm sure it made a big impact. I . . . I just want to remind you that our loved ones who've left us actually aren't that far away." Dilah watched as Little Bean's eyes filled with held-back tears. He couldn't see Tyrone's expression. "See, they're still beside us. They might be invisible, but they're still watching us, accompanying us, loving us . . . Um, I don't mean to imply anything by saying this. I hope it helps you. I won't bother you anymore. Good night."

Dilah saw that Tyrone was watching Little Bean's receding figure, sighing.

———◇———

The lake was enormous, and by the end of the next day, they still hadn't reached the far side. But the day after, they could make out a stone hill at the end of the lake, surrounded by thick mist. From afar, it looked like a gray giant with a long white beard, towering over the forest beyond. As they approached, they realized a waterfall cascaded down the stone hill, glittering in the sun and creating the beard-like mist they'd seen from a distance.

"This must be the waterfall Fario mentioned," Ankel said excitedly. "We've made it!"

"The spring of reincarnation!" the four exclaimed in unison, rushing toward the waterfall.

Dilah felt like he was running on air. Soon, their months of hard work would pay off. The spring of reincarnation was within reach, and so was their dream of becoming human.

The friends rushed over to the base of the falls—but the stone hill shrouded in mist wasn't on the ground . . . To their amazement, it was suspended in the air! Three smaller stone hills gently revolved around it. The hills were flat and sharp. Plants grew atop each one, sprouting in the crevices of the stones, thick vines dangling and skimming the ground.

The waterfall descended from the top of the central, largest floating hill, a glimmering crystal curtain. The water didn't seem to be affected by gravity in the normal way— it stretched out softly, like strands of silk. The waterfall gathered into a clear blue pool at the hovering foot of the hill, surrounded by thick white mist. The pool was so deep it appeared to be bottomless, and Dilah wondered if this was the source of the water flowing throughout the entire enchanted forest. They reveled in the extreme beauty of the suspended hill, spellbound, for several minutes.

Tyrone walked to the edge of the pool, unable to wait any longer. As he removed his hat and prepared to climb in, Dilah spotted three huge brown bears on the other side of the pool. Silently, one by one, they entered the water and disappeared beyond the waterfall, out of sight.

Undeterred, Tyrone plopped into the pool, his plump body creating a splash.

Dilah watched carefully. Would the three bears and Tyrone truly emerge from the pool as human beings? His heart was in his mouth as he waited and watched.

A moment later, Tyrone emerged from the water, took a deep breath, and stretched out both paws, studying himself.

"How come I haven't changed?" Tyrone asked, the three smaller floating hills circling above his head.

Dilah tried not to feel disappointed. Still, perhaps the magic wasn't instantaneous.

"It might take a while. Let's give it a try!" Ankel said to Dilah and Little Bean, diving in, his small yellow head bobbing in the water.

"What am I supposed to do? I—I can't swim . . ." Little Bean nervously said.

"Bathe in the shallow water. Don't go deep," Dilah advised him, wading in. The cold water eventually reached his neck, the bright sunlight painting golden ripples on his back. Little Bean cautiously stepped into the shallows, watching enviously as his three friends swam in the water, their silhouettes fluttering in the mist.

"How come we still haven't changed?" Tyrone repeated after a long while.

"Maybe—maybe we need to wait a little longer," Ankel said, somewhat awkwardly.

"Let's drink some of the spring water. Maybe it'll help," Dilah suggested.

And so they all gulped the sweet spring water, then floated in the pool, waiting for the magic to take effect. Nothing happened.

"What's going on?" Tyrone punched the water, making a huge splash.

The smile on Ankel's face froze, eventually melting away. Their bellies full of spring water, the four friends scrambled ashore like drowned chickens and lay on the huge rocks near the spring, basking in the sun, while the beautiful waterfall roared beside them.

"We failed, didn't we?" Ankel ruefully asked. "The spring of reincarnation doesn't exist after all."

"Even if it doesn't work out, I still love it here," Dilah said, smiling. "I'm glad we came."

"Thank you, Dilah." Ankel felt guilty. He'd been the one to suggest they look for the enchanted forest and the spring of reincarnation. He was touched that Dilah hadn't mentioned as much and had chosen to comfort him instead.

"I love it here too!" Little Bean said.

Tyrone said nothing—he was even quieter than usual.

"But where did those brown bears go?" Ankel asked suddenly. "I didn't see them anywhere when I was swimming around. Did you?"

Dilah and Little Bean shook their heads.

In the afternoon, they searched all around the waterfall but found no evidence of the bears at all.

"We should go," said Dilah, feeling dispirited. He glanced over at Tyrone. "I guess this is goodbye!"

"What?" Tyrone blinked.

"There's no spring of reincarnation. This is the end of our deal," Dilah said. "Isn't it?" He had no bad feelings for Tyrone—in fact, he felt sympathy for the troubled panda and wondered what had happened in his past. But ultimately, they had had a business arrangement: They had agreed to lead him to the spring, and Tyrone had offered protection in return.

Dilah was confused at the panda's obvious agitation at the thought of parting ways. "No!" Tyrone said. "You can't just leave me! I know you have another way. The rabbit told me everything."

Dilah glanced at Little Bean, who nodded sheepishly. "I told him all about the moonstone, Dilah. I'm sorry."

"Besides," Tyrone continued, "the road is dangerous. You still need me for protection!"

"Dilah, please, let's bring Tyrone!" Little Bean begged. "He wants this just as much as we do. And I really think he can help."

Dilah glanced over at Ankel, seeing his own doubt reflected in the weasel's eyes. "Little Bean," said Ankel, "I don't think it's a good idea. No offense, Tyrone, but we barely know you. You might steal the moonstone or the treasure—and who knows what else . . ."

"You're wrong. Tyrone would never do that," Little Bean protested.

"I won't betray you. You have my word," Tyrone promised, a trace of sadness in his eyes as he removed his battered bamboo hat. "I'll do whatever you say the entire time. I won't give you any trouble! I just want to turn into a human. You have to believe me."

Dilah stared into the panda's eyes for a few moments. He didn't know why, but Emily popped into his mind along with a crushing sadness. Then at last, he said, "OK. I believe you."

———◇———

That evening, they rested underneath a huge banyan tree. Tyrone fell asleep first, breathing heavily, followed by Little Bean, who emitted a high-pitched snore, then Ankel, who twitched as he dreamt. But Dilah tossed and turned, unable to fall asleep. After searching for months, they'd finally found the enchanted forest, and they'd also found the waterfall that, according to Fario's instructions, was what they were looking for: the spring of reincarnation. So . . . why hadn't they been reborn? Was the spring of reincarnation merely a rumor? Or had they been misinformed?

Dilah touched the moonstone hanging on the cord around his neck. Now following its light to Ulla's secret treasure was once again their only option. Makarov's warning rang out in his ears: *Whoever possesses it will suffer a fatal disaster.* Why was Ulla testing him? Did the patron saint of the Arctic foxes *want* him to die? Perhaps his whole quest was a big mistake . . . Despair clutched at his heart at the thought.

All of a sudden, he recalled what his mother had told him before she died: *Remember, when you've given up all hope, you can turn to our patron saint, Ulla, for guidance . . .*

Ulla, he thought, *if you're there somewhere . . . I need your help.*

He was turning his prayer over in his mind when sleep finally claimed him.

— ◇ —

In his dream, Dilah stood in a dark, shadowy cave.

"Dilah . . ." an ethereal voice called. The voice sounded as if it had drifted into Dilah's mind from somewhere far away.

A humanlike figure appeared in front of him in the darkness. The figure had its back to him and was cloaked and hooded, glowing faintly silver. "Who are you?" Dilah asked.

"I'm your patron saint, Ulla," the phantom figure said. "My dear child, why have you summoned me?"

Dilah's heart beat faster. Had he truly summoned the saint with his prayer? "My confusion is holding me back," he said, gathering his thoughts. "I need your guidance.

What should I do next? Follow the moonstone despite the danger? Or give up on my dream?"

"Follow the sage stone and seek out the wise one who can solve the puzzle." The voice and silver figure began fading. "Victory lies ahead, after a final test . . ."

———◇———

Dilah turned over as the dream faded, and he sunk into a deeper sleep, the leather parcel on his chest exposed, unaware of the huge black-and-white figure tiptoeing toward him.

It was Tyrone, and his paw was extended toward the little parcel containing the moonstone.

"Tyrone . . ." Little Bean mumbled.

Startled, the panda glanced at Little Bean in alarm. Little Bean's eyes were shut, and he began snoring again, muttering a few indecipherable words in his sleep from time to time. Tyrone hesitated, then resumed reaching for the parcel.

"Tyrone, please . . . we're friends. I believe in you," Little Bean grumbled, his eyes still closed.

Tyrone froze, glanced at Little Bean. After a moment,

he quietly returned to the place he'd been sleeping, lay back down, and closed his eyes. The corners of Little Bean's mouth turned up slightly.

———◇———

The next morning, after a good breakfast of purple berries, the four set off on their journey, carrying on beyond the waterfall and into the trees. Dilah confidently led the way toward the edge of the enchanted forest, a spring in his step. Both Ankel and Little Bean noticed there was something different about him.

"You're in a good mood," Ankel commented cautiously.

"Well—last night Ulla appeared to me! He told me to follow the moonstone and that success is close. We're going to make it!" Dilah said cheerfully. "I feel like a new fox."

"Ulla appeared to you . . . in a dream?" Ankel asked skeptically.

"That's right!" Dilah chirped. "But it wasn't just any dream—it was a *vision*. Trust me—it was all so clear, and I remember every detail. Ulla also said we'd find a sage who can help us solve the puzzle, whatever that means—"

"Dilah, why do you look bigger?" Little Bean interrupted.

"Huh?" Dilah asked, confused. He surveyed his friends. "Actually, I think all of *you* have gotten bigger . . ."

The four inspected one another. It was true: They'd all grown to twice their previous size!

"It must've been the spring beneath the waterfall, just like Fario said!" Little Bean marveled. "Wow!"

CHAPTER 6

Prophet Spring Valley

Dilah and his friends used the moonstone to guide them through the mist and lead them out of the enchanted forest. After that, they followed the moonstone's beam through a desolate plain, a cold marsh, and a vast area of farmland. Now they were beyond the edges of their map; only the moonstone could guide them.

Temperatures warmed up as they continued, and the air grew drier. They arrived at a barren desert. As they continued, they soon struggled for food and water. Hoping to find more fertile ground beyond the next horizon, they kept going—but instead plunged farther and farther into a barren yellow world. A large canyon opened up before them, and it seemed to Dilah as if the earth there had been split in two by a giant axe. It was a solemn place.

At dusk, the sun blinded them. Dilah's stomach grumbled; he felt as if he would faint from hunger. If they couldn't find food soon, they'd starve. As they trudged through the endless canyon, a flock of black birds streaked across the gray sky.

"Crows!" said Ankel hoarsely.

Hundreds of the birds hovered in the air like a cloud, changing formations and cawing. They whirled around to the bottom of the canyon like a tornado, circling something. The four friends continued to the center of the black tornado, where they found a pile of white bones streaked with traces of wet blood.

"What animals were these?" Dilah broke the silence first, his tone grim.

"Looks like a flock of sheep," Ankel said.

"Sheep? Here?" Tyrone asked.

"Maybe they got lost," Ankel suggested.

"Did the crows kill them?" Little Bean asked.

"No way. Crows are scavengers. They never attack live animals," Ankel said.

"Then how did they die?"

"They could've gotten lost and then starved to death, or maybe a different animal killed them," Ankel said uneasily.

"It's been two days since we've had anything to eat. We're in danger too." Dilah shuddered.

The canyon was a huge dry riverbed. It stretched out ahead of them, deep and never-ending. Then Dilah noticed movement nearby . . .

Clutching a potato bigger than her body, a jerboa struggled to jump as she approached the group, eyes fixed on the ground. She had yellow fur, a white belly, large ears, and a strong set of hind legs. Her tail was longer than her upper body and tipped in white.

"I'll talk to her and find out what's going on," Ankel whispered.

The jerboa turned her head as she noticed the friends for the first time. She froze, clutching the potato, clearly petrified but reluctant to drop her precious meal and run.

"Don't be scared," Ankel assured her. "We don't mean you any harm. May I ask how much farther we'll have to walk to get out of the canyon?"

The jerboa relaxed slightly. "Not far. You should be out in less than a day. There's a basin at the end of the canyon." The jerboa set down the potato, rolling her shoulders.

"Thank you. Can you tell me where we are?"

"Prophet Spring Valley."

"Prophet Spring Valley? What an odd name."

"It's called that 'cause there's a prophet who lives in the canyon. He supposedly knows everything. He can even predict the future!"

Could he be the sage? Dilah wondered, his ears pricking. He glanced over at Ankel, Tyrone, and Little Bean, certain they were thinking the same thing.

"How can we find the prophet?" Ankel asked.

"Follow the bottom of the valley until you come

to the tallest mountain at the edge of the canyon. He lives on top of the mountain." The jerboa pointed ahead.

"Excellent! Thank you very much!" Ankel said, beaming. His stomach rumbled.

"But be careful . . . There are wolves around," the jerboa warned.

Ankel gasped, his eyes widening. "Wolves?"

The jerboa nodded wisely. "They have a keen sense of smell and can pick up scents from long distances. I hope you won't run into any. But you should be careful." The jerboa picked up her potato and hopped away.

"Thank you for the warning!" Ankel called out to the jerboa's receding figure. He turned to his friends. "I'm guessing that's the fate that befell these poor sheep," he said grimly.

"We should go as far as we can tonight," said Dilah. "Let's get out of here as fast as possible."

———◇———

Night fell, the moon fat and round overhead. Dilah took out the moonstone to check their direction. The golden crescent spun vigorously in the bright moonlight before stopping, a beam of bright light pointing the way. Just then, they heard howls in the distance, rising and falling. Dilah's fur stood on end. He pictured pairs of red glowing eyes, ferocious teeth, and sharp claws glistening in the cold light.

"Yup, definitely wolves," Ankel said, his voice trembling.

"It's too dangerous to travel farther," Dilah decided. "Let's hide here among the rocks, sleep in shifts. We need to stay alert."

The howls continued through the night. When the morning sun slowly rose over the horizon, sprinkling golden-red light over the magnificent canyon, Dilah—who hadn't slept a wink all night long—heaved a huge sigh of relief. The wispy clouds in the sky glistened like fish scales.

The four friends decided to start early, eager to find the prophet right away. None of them had slept soundly. Little Bean couldn't stop yawning, Ankel's eyes were barely open, and Tyrone was even grumpier than usual.

They'd walked for a couple of hours when an animal appeared on a high rock overhead . . .

"Wolf!" Ankel cried.

"There's only one. Relax," Tyrone grumbled. "I can take him on."

"Maybe there are others nearby." Ankel shivered in fright. "Wolves aren't usually on their own."

"Don't panic," said Dilah. "Let's carry on for now—a bit quicker."

A few moments later, Dilah glanced back toward where they'd seen the wolf, sensing movement. He gasped. As Ankel had feared, a pack of around ten wolves emerged from the flying dust. And as the lead wolf caught Dilah's eyes, the pack started to run. They were incredibly fast.

"Go!" Dilah shouted to his friends at the top of his lungs. He bounded into a sprint, Little Bean and Ankel close at his heels.

"You three go first. I'll take them on!" Tyrone bravely turned around.

"Don't be a show-off—they'll tear you apart!" Dilah called, hesitating. "Now, hurry up!"

"You're . . . you're really worried about me?" Tyrone whispered, his eyes slightly watery.

"Now is hardly the time!" Dilah snarled. "Let's go!"

Dilah spun around and picked up his pace again, trusting Tyrone to follow. Ankel and Little Bean led Tyrone, dust swirling all around them in great sandy clouds.

After a while, Ankel and Little Bean showed clear signs of tiring and started to slow down. The wolf pack had no such problem; they were drawing closer and closer, one wolf close enough to snatch at Tyrone's fur. Bellowing, Tyrone paused mid-stride and punched him with the force of a thunderbolt. The wolf fell, tumbling in the sand. The others hesitated—clearly, they'd underestimated Tyrone.

Dilah soon realized the wolves had changed their tactics. Now wary of Tyrone's strength, they were in no rush to attack. Instead, they merely chased the four friends. This way, the wolves could take turns resting, while their prey had no choice but to exhaust themselves at full speed.

They ran for nearly half an hour more, until even Dilah's energy was dwindling, his vision starting to blur with exhaustion. Ankel's and Little Bean's mouths were wide open and panting—and then Ankel stumbled. The wolves saw their chance and sped up, unleashing an astonishing burst of power. Soon, they were right on their tails. Dilah glanced back. For the first time since they'd met, he saw Tyrone's eyes filled with fear. The burly lead wolf sprang up and stretched out his claws for the long-awaited feast, aiming for Tyrone . . .

But then, a mysterious golden light flashed above their heads.

"What?" Tyrone gasped breathlessly as the wolf who'd been so close to snatching at his leg fell back suddenly.

Dilah stopped and spun around in confusion as the sounds of pursuit faded. The lead wolf was rolling on the dusty ground, as if he'd been punched—but it wasn't Tyrone; he was staring wide-eyed, just as confused as Dilah was. Dilah watched in amazement as the next wolf appeared to hit a dense, invisible wall with a dull thud, bouncing and falling flat on his back. The next two wolves tried to stop but had picked up too much momentum and suffered an identical fate. The other wolves slowed. One tentatively rose on his hind legs and inspected the invisible wall, resting his front paws against its surface and trying to find out how high it was.

"What's . . . happening?" Little Bean gasped, clutching a stitch in his side.

The wolves whimpered. A scrumptious meal had

slipped away, and a few of their pack were badly injured.

A large, muscular wolf stood in the middle of the pack, glaring into the distance. Dilah and his friends followed his gaze . . .

A white fox stood majestically on a high cliff overlooking the canyon—a white fox, but standing on his hind legs. He had the posture, Dilah thought, of a human being. The fox-man gazed down on Dilah and his friends, clasping something shiny and golden.

Dilah realized they'd reached the bottom of the tallest mountain—exactly as the jerboa had mentioned. Could this strange fox-man be the prophet of Prophet Spring Valley?

Either way, the wolves knew they had no chance of defeating the otherworldly force protecting their prey, so they turned around and fled back toward the desert.

"You four, come on up!" an old and powerful voice called out from the clifftop. The words echoed throughout the valley, as though magnified by some magical power.

Dilah and the others caught their breath and walked toward the mountain, the canyon growing narrower and narrower, the ground cracked with long, deep fissures. The four friends trod carefully. A winding path wrapped around the mountain, leading to the peak, the mountain itself resembling a giant screw. The friends were even weaker with hunger and exhaustion by the time they finally reached the top, where a steep ledge provided a beautiful view of the desert valley below.

"At long last, you made it." An Arctic fox stood at the mouth of a cave, opposite the cliff edge. Dilah blinked. From afar, the fox had appeared to stand and act like a human—but the animal here was entirely fox-like. He was old, his voice kind and weathered, and he appeared to be blind, listening for Dilah's reply with closed eyes. "I've been waiting for you a long time."

"You knew we were coming?" Dilah asked, surprised. He shook his head. "Anyway, thanks for saving us just now."

"Saving you? I have no idea what you're talking about . . ."

"But I saw you—"

"Your eyes must've been playing tricks on you. It happens, out here in the desert."

Dilah knew the fox was right—the figure he'd seen had

been quite different from the one now standing in front of him. Yet, after only a few minutes of being in his presence, Dilah felt that this old white fox spoke with extraordinary eloquence and insight, his whole body exuding some sort of awesome power. He was more than he seemed.

"My name is Gulev," said the old fox.

"It's a pleasure to meet you. I'm Dilah. These are my friends: Ankel, Little Bean, and Tyrone."

Gulev smiled and nodded. "I bet you have a lot of questions for me. Am I correct? Come, follow me."

Dilah exchanged an impressed glance with his friends, and the four of them followed Gulev inside the cave. The circular space was large and bright, with a high ceiling dripping with stalactites. Natural openings led to further caves and passages beyond, suggesting a series of interconnected burrows. To Dilah's delight, Gulev guided them through the first cave into the next. Although the fox was blind, he appeared to have no trouble navigating through the network of chambers. The sunlight in the second cave blazed like fire, filtered through yellowish glittering stone. In the cavern beyond, the light was blue, reflecting from a beautiful waterfall, gurgles echoing from the walls.

Finally, Gulev led them into a milk-white arched cave with three circular skylights. As soon as they stepped inside, Dilah picked up on the scent of food. The four friends' bellies growled at the delicious smells. Dilah spotted stacks of food piled high in the cave's far corner: apples, nuts, pumpkins, carrots, potatoes, and exotic fruits.

Gulev smiled as he heard the rumbles of hungry stomachs. "Please, eat! In exchange for my predictions, animals often bring me more food than I can possibly manage alone." The friends hurried toward the corner for their first meal in days. As Dilah sank his teeth into a piece of delicious, ripe fruit, he felt he might cry with relief.

After a while, Ankel let out a huge burp. Little Bean sighed and wiped the juices from his mouth in satisfaction. Tyrone groaned, his belly like an inflated rubber ball.

"Thank you. If not for this delicious meal, I think we'd have starved here," Dilah said, curling his fluffy tail contentedly around his paws.

"You're most welcome. Have you had enough?"

"I'm stuffed to the gills," Little Bean said.

"Wonderful, wonderful. I know you four have suffered on your travels," Gulev said with concern. "And lost a lot along the way."

A surge of emotion welled up inside of Dilah. "We'll always have five members of our team," he blurted. "We wouldn't be here without . . ." A sharp pain pinched his heart as he remembered Emily's smile. He felt guilty that he hadn't done enough to protect her. He bowed his head.

"Dilah, don't be too hard on yourself," Gulev said in a soothing voice. "Only through pain can you truly learn how to love."

"But . . . she's left us forever!"

"Ah, that's not true, my dear child. She's never left you—and she never will."

Gulev's eyes were kind, and Dilah found he believed the old fox's words. "Thank you," he said quietly. Dilah cleared his throat. "We're here because . . . because, in a vision, I was told you can offer us some guidance."

But the old fox shook his head. "Now is not the time

for questions. Your friends are sleepy," he said. Dilah turned to find Little Bean's ears drooping, Tyrone leaning exhausted against the wall, and Ankel nodding himself awake. "Let's call it an early night!"

"But—"

"Look," Gulev insisted. "The sun is sinking. You've had a hard day. Allow yourself a chance to rest. Who knows— maybe you'll wake up tomorrow morning and suddenly everything will make sense!"

Despite the questions weighing on his mind, Dilah found he *was* incredibly tired. He joined his friends and lay down on the thick straw pile, Gulev's white silhouette disappearing into the darkness. The friends fell into a deep sleep as soon as their heads hit the straw.

CHAPTER 7

The Collar of Reincarnation

Dilah felt something drift past him and brush against his ears. He opened his bleary eyes, blinking. How much time had passed? At his side, Ankel, Little Bean, and Tyrone were all sweetly dreaming.

A ray of blue moonlight shone through the skylight overhead, and the arched cave seemed empty and silent. But, half squinting, Dilah saw a red fox standing at the mouth of the cave, glowing. His eyes widened. The red fox had big, bright eyes; long eyelashes; a pointed nose; slender limbs; and a large, gorgeously curved tail.

Who is she?

Dilah struggled to his feet. He ached everywhere. The red fox walked out of the cave, a few steps into the next one, turning back to gaze at Dilah, her eyes sparkling. Dilah followed.

The glowing red fox was like a lantern leading him through the intricate cave system. She turned left then right, then led Dilah down a twisting passage. She glanced back every now and then as if to check he was following, but she always kept her distance.

At last, they arrived in a huge arched cavern, the largest in the complex so far. On the floor of the cave, a glistening spring emitted a faint rainbow light that reflected onto the steep, uneven walls. The waters rippled, tiny bubbles emerging one after the other from the mouth of the spring. Half a stone bridge stretched from where Dilah stood.

At the end of the half bridge, the red fox turned around. Barely able to contain his excitement, Dilah stepped forward, but her image began to fade, and in seconds, she disappeared like mist.

Dilah's heart ached with fresh grief. How could an actual flesh-and-blood fox have evaporated in an instant? He studied the cave, wary of any danger, then carefully walked out onto the stone bridge, to the spot where the red fox had disappeared.

Peering at the cave walls, he realized they were covered in a series of red murals. *A story*, he thought wonderingly as he started to decipher the images. A fox hid in the trees, spying on a human. A fox and a human walked together. A fox sat in front of a magnificent palace. A fox stood atop a snowy peak searching for something, then gripped a stone in their mouth and walked over to a human cloaked in a cape and hood. A man picked up a stone, creating a glowing ring high in the air. A fox put on the ring of light and, as though breaking out of a cocoon, gradually transformed into a young human woman . . . The murals extended all over the stone walls. Dilah kept turning to take everything in until he glanced up and noticed a line of gilded script:

I was formed in the Arctic.

I bring hope and guide the way.

I'm filled with sky and moon,

on behalf of the northern night.

It all began with a love affair—a fox fell in love

with a human being.

It was a sad and beautiful love, one that touched

even the patron saint of the Arctic foxes.

More than a thousand years ago,

I was unearthed one fateful eve.

As soon as I was touched by Ulla's hand,

I took charge of the wheel of life and death.

From then on, desire was born . . .

I shall follow my new master,

in search of my other half.

Dilah removed the moonstone from around his neck, opened the leather parcel, and compared the poem on the cave wall with the one inscribed on the stone's leather parcel. They were nearly the same, except the poem on the wall had extra lines about a fox falling in love with a human. Likewise, the ceiling also contained a series of strange, picturelike symbols. Squinting, he closely compared them to the other inscription on the leather. Yes—it was the same Classical Animalese saying that was written on the leather. He remembered Ankel's translation, which had been the same as that of Grandpa Turtle, who Dilah had met near the start of his journey: *When you're lost, let the sky lead the way.*

What sort of cave was this—and how was it linked to the moonstone? Why was the inscription on the cave walls more detailed than the version on the moonstone's leather? Dilah's mind teemed with questions.

"Ah, young fox. I expected to find you here," Gulev called from behind Dilah. Dilah spun around, embarrassed that he'd found his way here without Gulev's permission. "Don't worry, child," the old fox said kindly as he stepped closer. "Were you also transfixed by her unmatched beauty?"

"I . . . Who was she?" Dilah asked, relieved Gulev wasn't angry at his presence here.

"Your guide was one of the first sages in the history of the white foxes: the fiery red fox Merla."

"What exactly is a sage?"

"A divine messenger. Sages pass on divine orders, and they help Ulla guard precious things," Gulev explained, joining Dilah on the stone bridge, his snowy fur reflecting the colorful lights from the spring.

Dilah nodded, then asked, "What's the deal with this poem? It's different from the one . . ." Dilah realized he hadn't actually told the sage about the moonstone. "I mean—"

"From the one on the moonstone you carry around your neck?"

Dilah felt his face warm under his fur. "How did you know?"

"I wouldn't be a very good prophet if I didn't know that, would I?" Gulev chuckled. "See, the poem on the leather is very old, but this version in the cave is the original. The missing two lines were lost as the legend circulated over the centuries."

Dilah scanned the unfamiliar lines again.

*It all began with a love affair—a fox fell in love
with a human being.
It was a sad and beautiful love, one that touched
even the patron saint of the Arctic foxes.*

"It's a love story?" Dilah said. "That's the reason for the moonstone's very existence?"

Gulev nodded. "Let me tell you the story. More than a thousand years ago, Merla, the first sage, was born in the Arctic fox clan. She was famous for her fiery red fur—unique among the white foxes. Her beauty and intelligence dazzled everyone she met. But that's not why she became a sage. She saved the foxes from extinction numerous times. She kept our species alive. As she grew increasingly revered among the foxes, the patron saint Ulla granted her the title of sage.

"But Merla had a peculiar habit: Like you, Dilah, she loved human beings."

Dilah felt his heart beat a little faster.

"She was fond of observing the humans who lived near the fox clan. And there was one in particular she loved to watch—a young hunter. The boy soon discovered that Merla often followed him. He grew very fond of her and treated her kindly. Over time, a special bond formed between them, and they grew up together, and at last, the unthinkable happened: Merla fell in love with this human.

"Merla was determined to marry the hunter, convinced he was her one true love, but she couldn't do so as a fox. So, she begged the patron saint to help her transform into a human girl. Ulla was enraged by her ridiculous request and refused. But Merla was determined. During the coldest snowstorm of the year, she sat at Ulla's palace gate for three days and three nights. Finally, Ulla was moved by Merla's persistence.

"Ulla gave Merla a near-impossible task to prove her commitment to the hunter: She had to search the mountains for a magical material she'd need in order to transform—moonstone. Merla succeeded against all the odds, but by the time she handed the moonstone she'd harvested to Ulla, she was close to death. As she lay dying, Ulla carved a fragment out of the moonstone to create . . . well, the talisman you now wear around your neck."

Dilah glanced down at the little package. To think, Ulla had actually touched it!

"As for the rest of the moonstone," Gulev continued, "Ulla used it to create a secret, powerful treasure, endowing it with the ability to help Merla realize her dream even as she died."

"Did Merla become human?" Dilah asked, his eyes wide. His story wasn't a love story, but even so, he felt immediately close to Merla, remembering how he had once watched the human family near his den. He hoped she had a happy ending.

"Of course. But as with all magic, there was a catch."

Dilah's heart sank.

"Merla didn't simply transform into a human of equivalent age to her fox body. Instead, her soul was reborn in the form of a human baby in a small Arctic village. At first, she didn't remember anything of her previous life— she grew up as an ordinary human girl. But when she turned sixteen, her memories flooded back.

"Of course, it had been sixteen years since Merla and the young hunter had known each other. She returned to his house and watched from the trees as she had once done as a young fox. The hunter was now nearly thirty years old, but as he set out for the forest one frosty morning, Merla realized it didn't matter—she loved him as she always had, and always would. She stepped out from the trees, heart leaping with joy, determined to reveal herself and the truth . . . but as she did, a beautiful woman emerged from the hunter's house, two young children at her side. She kissed the hunter on the lips."

"No!" Dilah gasped.

"The hunter was happily married, and Merla was heartbroken. As she turned away, the hunter noticed her on the edge of the clearing, and he called out to her. 'Do I recognize you from somewhere?' he asked. And when she said he didn't, that she was simply a lost traveler, he insisted on walking her to the road.

"As they walked, Merla gently asked the hunter questions about his life. She soon discovered that he was not the person she had known sixteen years earlier. She had been so convinced their souls were matched and immutable—but time had changed everything. Now, in truth, his true love was the woman he had married, not Merla. As they parted ways forever, Merla knew she had done the right thing in letting him go. But it didn't hurt any less." As Gulev spoke, the drawn-out, plaintive cries of wolves drifted in from outside, as though they too were sad for Merla's fate.

"What did she do next?" Dilah asked.

"No one knows, young fox. She disappeared into the human world, and so her story is lost. I hope and believe she found happiness at last." The old fox smiled sadly. "After that, Ulla hid the dangerous treasure somewhere safe, where only the bravest and most determined would find it. He gifted the fragment you hold to the white foxes, Merla's people, where it was passed down from generation to generation, always guiding the way to its hidden partner. But you know that already. And you know that the secret treasure is still writing its own mythology."

"So . . . the bigger part of this moonstone is the treasure I'm seeking?" Dilah asked.

"That's right. The moonstone treasure has the power to open the Gate of Reincarnation."

Dilah's mind was swirling with excitement and questions. Never had he felt so close to the thing he'd been seeking since his mother had died. "Gate of Reincarnation? What's that?"

"The link between the animal and human realms. All souls of animals who wish to become human must pass through this gate. There are many ways to open it. The spring of reincarnation is one—"

"The spring is real!" Dilah exclaimed. "But we were there. It didn't work! I mean, not in that way."

"Not every method works for every animal. The spring of reincarnation is specific to bears. The moonstone is available to every species."

Dilah nodded slowly, remembering how the bears they'd seen entering the spring had simply disappeared. Now he knew why. But then . . . "I don't get it." Dilah shook his head, confused. "I have to go through a gate— and the moonstone is the key? But didn't you just say the gate is in the spring of reincarnation?"

The old fox shook his head. "It's not a *physical* gate at all. Dilah, the typical law of life carries all creatures from birth to death . . . but its reverse process carries us from death to life. This is called reincarnation, and it happens naturally at the end of every creature's life. Do you follow?"

Dilah nodded slowly.

"Good. Now, listen, there is no magic in the world that can simply transform an animal into a human, preserving their original memory, because animals and humans have very different thoughts, behaviors, and instincts. Can you imagine how terrible it would be to force your present awareness into a human body? Why, you might not even be able to walk, let alone talk the way humans do! Remember what I told you about how Merla entered the human world? The catch?"

"She started as a baby . . ." Dilah whispered, starting to understand.

"Correct. Only by working with the natural method of reincarnation can we transform into human beings. Reincarnation naturally connects two very different species, washes away memories of the previous animal life, removes the animal coat, and cultivates a human self from infancy—and only in this way is there a true transformation into a human being. If you try to avoid reincarnation and force animals to become human . . . Trust me, it has been attempted, and you'll create horrible monsters."

Dilah felt a little dizzy as he started to grasp the truth. "On my journey, I met Makarov, the second elder of the Arctic foxes. He told me the treasure is a bloodthirsty thing, that it's a cursed, unlucky object, and that all foxes who find it will die. Is that true?"

"He's partly right. To a fox who doesn't understand the true magic of the treasure, it must seem cursed. For without death, how can there be rebirth?"

"Without death, how can there be rebirth?" Dilah repeated slowly. "So . . . basically, we're all going to die when we find the treasure," he said in a quieter voice. "Me and all my friends."

Gulev nodded, his face grave. "The real name of the secret treasure is the Collar of Reincarnation. After the reincarnation magic is activated, all of its owners die within three days, at which point their souls will pass through the Gate of Reincarnation and arrive in the human world as infants."

Dilah watched as a long string of tiny bubbles gurgled in the rainbow spring below. He was going to die on this quest. He was going to sacrifice everything of himself for the dream of becoming human. Not only him, but the friends who had joined and supported him too. Dilah imagined himself, Ankel, Little Bean, and Tyrone lying on the cold ground like his mother, like Emily, their bodies gradually fading into nonexistence, picked apart by crows and worms. Of course, from the time Dilah had embarked on his quest, he'd been prepared to die. In fact, he'd faced death innumerable times. But all in the hope of surviving—of continuing to fight for the treasure, for the dream of transformation, of changing the world. Now death itself was the destination, and a strange fear ate away at his heart.

"Death isn't something to be afraid of, Dilah," Gulev gently explained, as if he could read Dilah's mind. "To become the owner of the Collar of Reincarnation, you must overcome your fear of death. Even the divine phoenix must be burnt in order to be reborn from the ashes."

Dilah nodded slowly, accepting Gulev's advice. "But

the treasure . . . Are you sure it's a good thing?" he asked as new doubts arose in his mind. "It has brought about so much pain." Dilah thought of Carl, who'd resorted to fighting with Dilah's father—his former comrade in arms—over the moonstone. Because of the moonstone, his father had ended up dead; Carl had turned cruel; and Dilah's own brother, Alsace, had been expelled from the fox clan. Because of this treasure, the patriarch Jens and former head elder Gray had been killed, and the second elder Makarov had gone mad and left the Arctic . . . All these bad things had stemmed from this coveted treasure!

"The treasure itself is neither good nor evil. Power like that is defined by the intent of those who wield it . . . and only you know what is in your heart, little fox."

"And what of Makarov's son, Nicholas?" Dilah asked. "What became of his quest?"

"I met Nicholas here years ago. He was the last before you to seek the treasure," Gulev said. He sat down, his blind eyes appearing to stare up at shafts of moonlight breaking into the cave. "Nicholas thought the treasure was evil. He had decided to destroy the moonstone and Collar of Reincarnation, eliminating the cause of so much strife among his people.

"After he found the Collar of Reincarnation, he made a bold choice. Holding the moonstone in his mouth and wearing the collar, he leapt from the top of a mountain into an abyss, hoping that these two treasures would disappear from the world with him," Gulev said, his voice somewhat sad.

"But the moonstone . . ." Dilah glanced down at the package around his neck. "It's still here. His plan failed," he said blankly.

"As I warned him it would. But in failing, Nicholas allowed your dream to live on," Gulev said. "And now, instead of trying to destroy Ulla's gift, you have a chance to use it for good."

Dilah let out a deep breath. Gulev was right. He had to stay true to his path, whatever faced him—a path he'd followed from the very start and that he believed to be good and honest. He had to stare down his fear of death, force his doubts about the treasure out of his mind. What mattered was what was in his heart. Victory was near. He silently renewed his vow to find the Collar of Reincarnation—Ulla's secret treasure.

"I can see you're nearly ready to embark on the last leg of your journey, but before you leave this place, I'll tell you one more thing," Gulev said. "Not every Arctic fox is fit to become the master of the Collar of Reincarnation."

"Even if I find it, I could still fail?" Dilah asked, feeling a little deflated.

"I'll let you in on a little secret, Dilah. In order to become human, you must possess the five human attributes: faith, wisdom, kindness, courage, and love. The Collar of Reincarnation will test you to see whether you possess these attributes before allowing you to pass through the Gate of Reincarnation."

"But I don't think I have all of those attributes—maybe one or two . . ." Dilah said, feeling slightly panicky.

"Don't forget about your friends. They can help you collect all five attributes. Along the way, you've helped one another through thick and thin. Together, could you already have everything you need? Think about it."

Images of Dilah's friends flashed through his mind like lightning. Ankel undoubtedly possessed rare wisdom. Little Bean had true kindness. Tyrone . . . well, he was the newest of Dilah's friends, but although he was quiet, he was a fierce protector. Perhaps he represented love. Dilah himself . . . well, he'd had the conviction to travel all alone from the North Pole, sticking to his journey no matter what had stood in his path. Perhaps he was the one with the most faith. That left one attribute . . .

"If Emily had survived," Dilah said, bowing his head, "she would have been our courage. But now I'm not sure where we'll find that."

Gulev smiled kindly. "If you seek a glimpse of the future, I think I can do you a small favor, child. This is no ordinary spring." He signaled with his nose down into the rainbow waters below the half bridge on which they stood. "The powerful magic of time flows within it. Past, present, and future all lie in its waters—it's how I guide the animals who visit me for help. So, gaze into the spring and concentrate on your question. We will find some answers there."

Dilah walked to the very edge of the bridge and peered over the spring, startled to see his magnified reflection. The Arctic fox in the water gave him a strange feeling. He was no longer the scrawny little cub who'd left the North Pole—he was now a big, strong Arctic fox. He looked like his father. Like Alsace. Only he was even bigger, after his swim in the enchanted spring.

Following Gulev's instructions, Dilah gazed intently at the water, focusing on the fifth attribute: courage. Where would he find it? As he watched, holding the question in his mind, large bubbles sprang up through the spring; the water was boiling and gurgling! The rainbow light grew intense, and multicolored beams surged wildly throughout the cave. Dilah stepped backward, alarmed.

Then, all of a sudden, the myriad colors converged into a sky blue glow, the cave dimmed, and the bubbles died down.

Dilah stepped closer to the spring again—except now it was more like a long, calm pool—a mirror carved out of sapphire, emitting a faint blue light. Dilah's reflection slowly faded away. He gasped, but was rooted to the spot. In the glassy surface of the water, he saw a roiling pitch-black sea, the sky covered in dark clouds, lightning flashing, wind and rain whipping against the surface of the waves. Dilah could practically hear the thunder and feel the cold vapor from the sea.

What was this vast, churning ocean? What did it mean? He'd find courage in the sea?

Now the image of the ocean had faded, and the surface of the water was boiling again, bubbles rising from the blue mouth of the spring. The water turned gold and glowed brightly. For a few moments, Dilah and Gulev were bathed in warm light. When the water calmed, Dilah was surprised to see nine big bushy tails briefly flash across the golden mirror, vanishing into his own reflection as the rainbow colors returned. He blinked. Had he imagined that?

He turned to Gulev. "I saw the sea," Dilah said, puzzled. "A big, stormy sea. But I'm not sure what it means."

"It's simple. You'll encounter a friend with the fifth attribute at sea," Gulev said.

"Really?" Dilah was confused but, for now, set his doubts aside. "I—I also saw something else, but I'm not sure if I was mistaken . . ."

"What was it?" Gulev quietly asked, his blind eyes closed.

"I think I saw nine fox tails flash by in the water. I could be wrong, though. It was so quick."

"Anubis? How could it be him?" Gulev was obviously shocked, his voice tinged with grave concern. "Dilah, please listen. If you see a nine-tailed fox on your travels, you must tread carefully indeed. Anubis is an ancient white fox sage. If he's the one guarding the Collar of Reincarnation . . ." He shook his head.

"Will I have to fight him to get the collar?"

"He has nine lives, Dilah. He won't be cowed by force. Instead, you'll have to use reason, little fox," Gulev said, his grave face blooming into a friendly smile. Dilah couldn't help but grin back.

"I understand. Thank you very much for your advice." Dilah was extremely grateful to the wise fox, whom he respected from the bottom of his heart.

"All right, child. It's getting late. Get back to bed! You and your friends will be setting off early tomorrow morning, I'm sure."

After saying goodbye, Dilah found his way back by tracking his own scent through the moonlit caves. He gazed fondly at his friends for a moment—each one of them sound asleep in the straw—and at last he crept into their midst, curled his long fluffy tail around him, and fell into a deep, dreamless slumber.

———◇———

Dilah woke up to a crunching noise. His eyes fluttered open. The first rays of morning sunlight streamed through the circular skylight overhead. Ankel and Little Bean sat next to the pile of food in the corner, chomping happily. Tyrone lay on the straw with his eyes open, clutching the bamboo hat on his belly with one paw. Dilah stood up and shook the straw out of his coat.

"Let's set off as soon as we've eaten," he said brightly.

"What?" Ankel was taken aback. "Didn't we just find the sage?"

"Yeah. Gulev hasn't even explained the mysteries!" Little Bean chimed in.

"He doesn't need to. He told me everything last night while you three were snoring," Dilah said merrily. "I'll explain on the way."

Once they'd eaten and drunk their fill, the four friends stepped outside to the desert clifftop, noticing Gulev waiting for them nearby.

"Good morning!" Dilah called out.

"Good morning!" Gulev said, smiling.

"We're heading out. Thank you so much for your care and help. We loved it here! I wish we could stay." Suddenly, Dilah really didn't want to leave. The beautiful dry cave system with its abundant food and soft straw felt more like home than anywhere he'd been since his family den. And kind old Gulev . . . If Dilah had known his grandfathers, he imagined they might've been a little like Gulev. In his presence, Dilah felt truly safe.

But he couldn't abandon his quest. Not when they were so tantalizingly close to the end.

"All right, child, don't feel bad saying goodbye to an old codger like me," Gulev said kindly, his eyes closed.

"This might be the last time we'll see each other," Dilah said, sad at the thought.

"Oh, Dilah, take that back," Gulev said, smiling. "We'll meet again."

"When?" Dilah hadn't expected this.

"It's up to you."

"What do you mean?" Dilah asked. But the old fox simply shook his head.

"You'll see."

"OK, then . . . see you soon!" Dilah said.

"See you soon!" Gulev replied cheerfully. And in a quiet voice, he added to Ankel, "In my next letter, I'll tell your grandfather what a fine young weasel you've turned into, little one."

Ankel blinked. "You know my grandfather?" But Gulev just smiled mysteriously. His friends had started on the winding path down the mountain, and Ankel hurried to follow.

At the bottom, Dilah gazed over his shoulder and glimpsed a white spot on the edge of the golden cliff, watching from afar. Smiling, he ran and caught up with his friends.

As they walked, Dilah told Ankel, Little Bean, and Tyrone everything that had happened in the magical cave the previous night.

"Wow! So the treasure is the Collar of Reincarnation— and such a tragic and beautiful story behind it!" Ankel sighed.

"Yes. Now things make a lot more sense," Dilah said.

"No wonder those three bears disappeared right under our noses. They went right through the Gate of Reincarnation!" Tyrone huffed.

"I wish we could've spent a few more days in the enchanted forest," Little Bean said wistfully.

"I wish we could've stayed longer with Gulev," Dilah replied. "But our adventure won't wait! Come on, let's pick up the pace."

CHAPTER 8

A Farce

Dilah, Ankel, Little Bean, and Tyrone ran, the yellow earth receding behind them. In a day and a half, consulting the moonstone's beam at night, they'd left behind the barren valley and arrived at a large grassy basin. A warm and gently humid spring breeze grazed their faces. Patches of green sprouted from the dry yellow grass, and the willow trees along the roadside burst with emerald buds. Winter had quietly disappeared at last.

"Gulev said we'd meet our fifth companion at sea," Dilah said. "The air smells different . . . Do you think we're getting close?" The setting sun, like a great ball of fire, fell toward the horizon, gilding the four friends in gold.

"Yes. The vegetation is lusher," Little Bean observed. "We must be near water."

"Dilah, are you sure you're not mistaken?" Ankel narrowed his eyes. "The sea you thought you saw in the spring was probably an illusion created by the ripples in the spring itself."

"I'm not mistaken. The water wasn't even rippling at that point—I told you," Dilah said, irritated by Ankel's skepticism. "I definitely saw the sea. *And* I saw a nine-tailed fox. Or do you think that was an effect of the water ripples too?" Dilah asked sarcastically.

But Ankel either missed or ignored Dilah's annoyance. "A nine-tailed fox! That is seriously cool," Ankel repeated in awe.

"What *exactly* is a nine-tailed fox?" Tyrone interjected.

Ankel cleared his throat and puffed out his chest. He

loved to be asked academic questions! "The nine-tailed fox, Tyrone, is one of the ancient legendary beasts—powerful and ever changing. Each tail represents a life, meaning it has nine lives."

"What did Gulev make of your vision, Dilah?" Little Bean asked.

"Well . . . I think this nine-tailed fox, Anubis, might be guarding the treasure," Dilah sighed.

"Oh no! How can we defeat a creature with nine lives?" Little Bean asked anxiously.

"That's easy—killing him nine times should do it," Tyrone said coldly.

"Gulev said we shouldn't try to defeat him by force," Dilah retorted. "He said we should try reasoning with him."

The big panda snorted derisively, and the group fell into silence.

Before they knew it, weeks had passed, and the temperature was rising as spring shifted toward summer. The air grew humid, and Dilah started to feel sand and gravel mixed in with the earth beneath his paws. Finally, the four friends arrived at a rocky promontory overlooking the ocean. Dilah was glad to hear the whoosh of the waves and feel the cool sea air in his fur. He was reminded of the early days of his journey and his friend Egg, the seal.

As night fell, Dilah checked the moonstone, and they followed its beam down toward the sea. Then, to the animals' horror, they realized the moonstone was pointing straight toward a quiet seaside town.

"Humans!" Little Bean squeaked in terror as a few tall shapes moved among the houses.

Dilah tried to be brave as he gazed at the settlement. The town was shrouded in quiet moonlight. The air was fresh, and the scenery was pleasant. There were stately villas everywhere, big white boats in the bay, and even shiny cars driving in and out of town.

"Let's wait until it quiets down," Dilah said. "Hopefully, the moonstone will lead us straight through and out the other side."

As night deepened, lights started to go out. The residents of the town were largely in bed.

"Let's go," said Dilah, hoping none of the humans peeked out of their windows to spot an Arctic fox, a panda, a weasel, and a rabbit—each twice their species' usual size!—wandering down their streets. The four friends entered the town cautiously, keeping to the shadows and finding the sensations of paving stones strange under their paws.

After half an hour or so, they arrived in a silent, empty square. Rays of moonlight shone onto a tinkling fountain with a statue of a mermaid in the square's center. Dark green holly bushes divided the square into uniform grassy areas with paved pathways between. Trees neatly lined both sides of the path like soldiers. Dilah was struck by how humans controlled and regimented nature until it felt as human-made as one of their stone houses.

Dilah and his friends climbed up the steps to the fountain and drank from its waters. The mermaid's expression was serene in the moonlight. Ankel stood on his tiptoes and scouted out the area, then nodded to Dilah to signal the all clear. Dilah removed the leather parcel from his neck and opened it beneath the moonlight. The golden crescent in the center of the moonstone spun, stopped, and pointed their way forward. Ankel picked up the moonstone and set it down on the stone steps, studying it closely, and then moved it to the stone bench beside the road, continuing to inspect it. Suddenly, he jumped up, spluttering and pointing at the beam, dancing from foot to foot.

"What is it?" Dilah asked, gazing at the familiar light. "Wait a minute . . . Has the direction changed?"

"Yes! The crescent turned around sharply!" Ankel shouted. "Before, it was pointing along the coastline. Now it's pointing toward the sea!"

"Hooray! At last, we must be so close!" Little Bean said happily.

"I know where it is!" drifted a sweet voice from above.

Caught off guard, the four friends glanced up. A snow-white Persian cat was hiding in a pruned tree overhead. Her large amber eyes shone in the moonlight.

She'd have seen everything from up there as they consulted the moonstone.

"Who are you?" Dilah asked warily.

"Oh, my darlings, don't be afraid. And please pardon my rudeness. Allow me to introduce myself. I'm a feline aristocrat, the cream of the crop! I'm a good friend of humans too. My name is Opal." She gently raised a paw in greeting.

"Why are you hiding up there?" Tyrone asked tetchily. "Were you spying on us?"

"On the contrary. I was here first, minding my own

business, when you four creatures ventured into my garden." Opal batted her lashes and yawned. "But if you don't want me to help you . . ."

"Help us with what?" Dilah asked.

"Help you," Opal began, then deftly leapt down, landing on the ground without a sound, "find the treasure! What else?"

The Persian cat had a fat, round face that had a squashed quality, and her huge amber eyes reminded Dilah uncomfortably of Carl's. She was all white, was outrageously fluffy, and wore a string of pearls around her curiously short neck as a collar, a little golden token hanging from its center. She was a pet, Dilah concluded. A human's creature.

"You say you know the treasure that we're searching for?" Ankel asked warily.

"Of course. I've seen it with my own eyes. It's no ordinary treasure," Opal said, narrowing her eyes at Ankel.

"What kind of treasure is it, then?" Dilah asked.

"I'm not sure, sweetness. I didn't get a very good look.

But from what I glimpsed, I think it's something to wear around your neck."

Dilah's scalp tingled. Could it really be the Collar of Reincarnation? "What makes you so sure that the thing you saw is what we're looking for?" he asked.

"Isn't it obvious?" the cat purred smoothly. "The magical gem on your chest, it's pointing in the direction of the treasure, isn't it? Well, it just pointed toward my mistress's house, on the bay. I simply put two and two together."

Dilah and his friends exchanged hopeful glances. Dilah remembered what Gulev had told him—how Nicholas had thrown himself into an abyss, hoping to destroy the treasure forever. Well, humans were known for their adventurous spirits. Could the treasure have been retrieved by a human and brought to this place? The thought that they could finally hold the Collar of Reincarnation set his pulse racing with mingled excitement and fear.

"Where is it?" Tyrone asked Opal. He wasn't one to beat around the bush.

"Oh, sweetie, I can't simply tell you that. What would be in it for me?" Opal said, her voice honeyed.

"Well . . . what do you want?" Dilah asked.

"Why, it's very simple. I'll take you to the treasure, but once you have it, you give me your pretty stone," Opal said, licking her paw and running it over her immaculate fluffy white ears.

"Stone? You mean the moonstone?" Dilah was taken aback.

"Indeed. I've taken quite a fancy to it. I love beautiful things, and so does my mistress. This will be a wonderful addition to her collection—and compensate for the loss of the other treasure."

"Dilah, what do you think?" Ankel asked.

"Once we find the treasure, we don't need the moonstone." Dilah gazed down at the heavy moonstone on his chest with mixed feelings. He wasn't sure how he'd feel without it . . . but then, once he was reborn as a human, the stone would magically return to the white fox clan, wouldn't it? Or if not, perhaps that was a good thing—perhaps giving it to Opal to keep safe was the best way to protect the other white foxes from further strife, for now. "OK," he said, glancing at the fluffy cat. "We have a deal."

"Marvelous!" Opal cried out. "I'm so pleased! And I think it's only fair that I hold the moonstone while I lead you to the treasure—simply as a precaution, you understand."

"You—" Ankel cried out, exasperated.

"What is it, dearest weasel? We're working together, aren't we? Don't you trust me?" She batted her eyelids.

"It's OK. I'll give it to her." Dilah removed the leather parcel from around his neck and held it toward Opal. What did it matter who held the moonstone, now they were so close? Besides, it was four against one, and if she tried to run, he was certain he could catch her. Opal was a pampered house cat, while Dilah was hardened by long months of travel.

"Excellent," said Opal, slipping the package over her neck next to her pearl collar and carefully tightening the cords so the moonstone didn't drag on the ground. "Let's be on our way. We must arrive before morning when my mistress wakes up."

"Dilah, I don't want to question your judgment . . . but could this be a trap?" Ankel whispered to Dilah as they followed the fluffy cat through the streets toward the sea.

"Don't be afraid. I'm here," Tyrone said, cool and collected.

Dilah nodded. "We're a team. Opal is only one cat. We've got this!"

Ankel looked doubtful but didn't say anything more.

The group followed a small road to the outskirts of the town and finally wound up a hill covered in red-tipped weeds. At the top, the boundless moonlit sea glittered into view once more. The four friends and Opal stopped to admire the view.

"Isn't it a glorious night?" Opal said in her posh, silky voice. "But let's hurry, we don't have long until dawn!"

They started walking along a small cobblestone drive. At the end of the drive was a large villa, its pale exterior glowing softly in the moonlight.

The house had a wide veranda, covered in fragrant flowers, overlooking a small, elegant garden with a beautiful angel statue in the center. A sharp drop down led to the beach and the sea. Dilah could tell the views from the house would be spectacular.

Wow—Opal really did live in luxury!

Opal rushed toward the veranda doors, but Dilah and his friends followed warily, hanging back as they approached. Dilah had only been inside a human house once, and he didn't think Little Bean, Tyrone, or Ankel ever had . . .

"Listen, my darlings," whispered Opal, urging the friends closer. "You have to be super quiet and super fast, all right? My mistress is a light sleeper. The weasel and I can use the cat flap and unlock the door. The rest of you wait here."

Opal slipped in through the cat flap, closely followed by Ankel. Dilah, Little Bean, and Tyrone waited nervously outside.

"Do you really think we can trust her?" Little Bean whispered.

"If the treasure is inside, I don't see that we have a choice," Dilah said.

Tyrone grumbled discontentedly.

Dilah shifted, his tail flicking, hoping Ankel was all

right. Could a cat kill a weasel? He didn't think so, and Ankel was almost the size of a cat now, anyway. Even so, Dilah gulped, his throat dry as he hoped he hadn't sent his friend into mortal danger.

Thankfully, moments later, the door clicked open. A beam of moonlight streamed through the crack in the door, lighting Opal's amber eyes.

"Enter, my dear guests," Opal whispered grandly. Behind her, Ankel was already admiring the room, his mouth open in amazement.

Dilah, Little Bean, and Tyrone sneaked inside. "Whoa . . ." whispered Dilah as he gazed around the interior. The ceiling was adorned with ornate reliefs, a gigantic chandelier hanging from the center. Several comfortable, luxurious seats and an end table inlaid with gold were positioned in the middle of the room. A vase of fresh flowers and an exquisite china tea set were carefully arranged on the end table.

"As much as I appreciate your admiration," Opal whispered, "we ought to be getting on."

Opal guided the four friends down a hall and into a

small room, opening the door by standing nimbly on her hind legs and pressing her paws against the handle. Once everyone was inside, Opal shut the door and switched on the light, hopping on Tyrone's shoulders to flick the switch with her nose.

Dilah blinked in the sudden bright light. As his eyes adjusted, he realized they were standing in a storage room. A large glass-doored cabinet was filled with glass bottles. A metal rail was crammed with fat mink coats. Antique vases of various styles stood gathering dust on a huge polished wooden shelving unit.

But Opal was heading for a small cabinet in the corner. She flexed her claws and carefully spun a small dial. A click sounded, and the cabinet opened, revealing a gold jewelry box.

"It's in here," Opal said smoothly, nudging the box open with her nose. "Why don't you take a look?"

Dilah and his friends eyed the box with excitement. Finally, the long-awaited moment had arrived! Impatient, Tyrone grabbed the jewelry box and dumped everything onto the floor with a loud clatter.

"You idiot!" Opal hissed, darting anxiously toward the door. The ties of the moonstone pouch had fallen loose around her neck.

A loud *meow* sounded in the hallway, and Opal froze, her mouth tight, teeth bared.

Dilah silently signaled for Ankel, Little Bean, and Tyrone to search through the box. He watched Opal closely as the door swung open.

"I knew it was you slinking back, you lowly mixed breed!" the cat in the hallway—a beautiful blue-gray Chartreux with shining yellow eyes—hissed loudly.

"Why do you have to mess everything up?" Opal hissed back, her eyes large and fierce. Her voice was now completely devoid of sweetness. "Before you came along, everything was perfect!"

"Not for Mistress. Or she wouldn't have wanted me, would she?" the Chartreux retorted smugly.

Opal's hackles rose as she crouched down, ready to pounce. "But guess what, sweetie? I've got something that will make Mistress love me more. Soon it'll be *you* who's out on the street!" Her entire body trembled with rage.

The blue-gray cat let out a low growl, matching Opal's stance. "Mistress loves me more! She always will! You should stay out on the street where you belong."

"Meow! Mee-owww!" replied Opal in wordless rage, swiping a surprisingly fast and sharp-clawed paw toward her enemy.

"Dilah!" Ankel hissed from the storeroom. "There's nothing here. Most of it isn't even real gold," he said.

"This is definitely a trap," agreed Tyrone with a low growl.

Dilah's heart sank at the realization—and all of this was his fault. His eagerness to believe they'd found the treasure had led him to trust Opal against his better instincts. He turned his attention to the hall. The two cats tussled and hissed, colliding with a small side table, which sent a vase crashing to the floor.

If the cats' mistress wasn't awake yet, she would be now!

"Quick!" said Dilah.

The four friends hurried out of the storage room and into the hallway, flashes of white fluff and lean blue fur scuffling on the parquet floor farther down. Screeches pierced the air. The floor was strewn with tufts of fur, vase shards, and scattered fake pearls.

Opal's collar had broken. And if that had broken . . . Dilah scanned the floor desperately. They couldn't leave without the moonstone!

An upstairs light switched on, spilling a yellow glow into the living room, where the cats struggled on, oblivious. The friends heard footsteps padding along the upstairs hallway toward the stairs.

And suddenly, Dilah spied it: The moonstone was on the floor, half-hidden under the flowers from the vase. He quietly snatched it up, then motioned to his friends that it was time to leave—fast! They bolted past the fighting cats, out of the villa, onto the veranda, and into the blessed darkness of the garden.

Dilah glanced over his shoulder, back toward the brightness of the living room. He couldn't see Opal, but the human mistress had gathered the gray-blue cat into her arms and was kissing it softly on the head.

"Come on," said Ankel. "We need to go. I don't want to deal with Opal again."

"She tricked us," Little Bean agreed.

"I shouldn't have trusted her," Dilah said as they started to descend the hill, wordlessly heading down toward the sea.

"It's not your fault," Tyrone grumbled.

Dilah wondered whether Opal was all right. She had tricked them, yes. But it sounded like she had simply wanted to win back the affections of the mistress she loved. He couldn't help feeling a little bad for the cat. For all her airs and graces, she'd clearly fallen on hard times and was desperate for a way out.

———◇———

Dawn broke as the friends traipsed down to the sandy beach.

"Should we rest awhile?" Tyrone suggested.

But Dilah shook his head. "Ankel was right. We should get away from here—too many humans." *And cats*, he added to himself.

The damp sea air tousled their fur, and the cool waves, tinged crimson by the sunrise, washed the dirt and sand from their paws. Seagulls hovered in the sky, crying out in their clean bright voices. The moon hovered weak and low, but Dilah opened his leather parcel nonetheless, hoping to catch a glimpse of their direction before the day grew too bright. The moonstone glowed faintly. Once the spinning stopped, the beam pointed over the sea.

Now they faced a new problem: How were they supposed to continue their journey on water?

"Remember earlier—didn't we see a harbor?" Ankel said. "I think there were some boats there . . ."

"Of course!" Dilah was glad of his friend's quick mind. "OK, let's head over now. I think it was this way."

They walked along the beach as the sun rose, yawning with exhaustion, until they reached the harbor. The day had barely started, and everything was quiet. At last, it appeared fate was on their side.

On the edge of a pier of yachts and luxury sailing boats, they found a worn-out dinghy, unattended and perfect for the four of them. Untying the ropes, they stole the boat and sailed out into the unknown water.

CHAPTER 9

The Fifth Attribute

Dilah and his friends had been sailing two whole days without food, the supplies of fresh water they'd found in the boat nearly exhausted. Now it was their second night on the water, but there was no chance of sleep tonight. Thick clouds rolled like a huge relief sculpture in the dark sky. The wind grew stronger and stronger, and the sea began to rage, the wind whipping the spray against the tiny sailboat.

A storm was coming.

The little dinghy was rocked violently on the churning waters. Ankel shouted over the howling wind for Tyrone to lower the sail.

The four friends clung to the boat, rising and falling with the waves, utterly directionless. Dilah wondered if this was, at last, how his epic journey would end—so close to their destination. Lightning flashed and thunder crackled as pea-sized raindrops rattled onto the ocean's surface.

Giant waves beat against the boat, surging over the sides. The four friends were quickly drenched from head to toe, and completely helpless as they clung close to one another and the groaning boat. The dark sea would swallow them up, Dilah thought, their dreams and hopes along with their lives. Everything felt so small now in the face of nature's fury.

Lightning sizzled in the sky. In the split-second flash, through the wind and rain, Dilah glimpsed a strange silhouette . . . a huge black fox towering motionlessly above the waves. Dilah frowned through the deluge, certain

he'd been mistaken. But then more lightning flashed—and Dilah gasped. An island with a craggy fox-shaped mountain stood outlined against the storm! Hope rose up in his heart.

"Can you see that island?" Dilah shouted to his friends. The little boat was half-filled with water. Soon they were going to sink. "We'll have to swim!"

"But I can't swim through these big waves!" Ankel yelled, his face a rictus of fear.

"It's our only chance! The boat won't last much longer."

"What about Little Bean? He can't swim at all!" Ankel said.

"I'll help him—you two take care of yourselves!" Tyrone called out. Lightning exploded behind him, lighting up the sky, and there was a peal of thunder.

"All right," Ankel called, visibly steeling himself. "See you on the island!"

A giant wave gathered force nearby. It was now or never.

"JUMP!" Dilah's voice shot through the storm like a bullet. The four friends took deep breaths, then leapt into the bottomless sea, Little Bean clinging to Tyrone's fur. Behind them, their poor little boat smashed to pieces as the huge wave tumbled down on top of it.

Dilah dived down under the wave until his lungs burned. He felt as though every cell in his body was battling against the cold water—as if, bit by bit, the sea was draining away his heat and life like a hungry beast. He rose up for air and—to his relief—noticed his friends bobbing up and down nearby, struggling toward the fox-shaped island.

Ankel led the way, Dilah following close behind. Glancing back, he saw Tyrone fighting to keep afloat with Little Bean clinging to his neck. Little Bean's eyes were wide with fear, his long ears stuck to his back.

The sea heaved, sunk down, and Dilah glanced up, his own eyes wide too. A large wave towered over the friends, and as it crashed down, Dilah felt himself tumbling over and over in the spray, unsure which way was up. When he finally found the surface, gulping for air, Tyrone was nearby, frantically searching the water. Dilah's worst fear had come to pass: Little Bean had lost his grip on the panda.

"I can't find him!" Tyrone roared in frustration.

A bolt of lightning lit the ocean, and they saw a tiny shape struggling on the water's surface.

"I see him!" Dilah shouted. He had to get Little Bean safely ashore before the next wave! He swam over, pushing against the current, and grabbed Little Bean at the nape of his neck. The rabbit hung limp in his mouth and felt impossibly heavy as Dilah urged his exhausted body to swim toward the island.

"Dilah!"

Help was at hand. Tyrone swam near, gently removed Little Bean from Dilah's grip, and hoisted the rabbit onto his back. He swam on toward the shore, leaving Dilah to follow. But Dilah's energy was drained. He tried to keep up, but he couldn't. As he watched Tyrone swim farther and farther away, toward the island, Dilah felt his limbs grow numb, his vision blurring.

Yet another large wave bulged in the water nearby. This time, Dilah was too weak to take a deep breath in preparation. Before he knew it, the wave was crashing over him, and he was sinking into the ink-dark water. He had no air, no sense of direction. As he opened his mouth instinctively, water gurgled into his lungs.

The moonstone. He felt the crush of failure even as his vision started to fade. After everything he'd been through, everything he'd put his friends through . . . everything was lost. And the moonstone . . . If only he'd managed to pass it on to one of his friends, they could have continued the quest without him.

As his consciousness faded, Dilah sensed a dark something rushing toward him at breakneck speed, striking him like a football and pushing him upward . . .

———◇———

Dilah felt as if he'd been dreaming for a long time . . . What had happened in his dreams? Suddenly, he couldn't remember. Dilah felt soft ground under his body and warm sun on his fur. He smelled the salty air, heard the cries of seagulls. Was this a dream too? He slowly opened his eyes. A familiar shape poked through the glare of the sunlight.

"Old chap, you finally woke up!"

As he blinked, the round white head came into focus.

Grinning, his old pal Egg held out a large flipper to greet Dilah.

"Egg!" Dilah cried, springing to his feet and clapping his paw against Egg's palm. The two old friends smiled at each other, wordless with joy. The seal had helped Dilah discover how to use the moonstone, but they had parted ways soon after, as Egg had gone in search of his parents. Sitting on the sand behind Egg were Ankel, Tyrone, and Little Bean, smiling in the sunshine. The storm had passed, and everyone was safe. Dilah's heart lifted.

"You saved my life!" he said to Egg.

"And you saved mine," said Little Bean to Dilah.

"So did I," Tyrone pointed out.

Ankel laughed. "I think we're all even at this point, aren't we?"

Dilah's heart felt as warm and bright as the sun.

"If not for the stone on your chest, I wouldn't have recognized you," Egg said, smiling. "Old chap, you've grown so much that dragging you along behind me almost killed me!" He stuck out his tongue. Like Dilah, he was bigger than before, but no less playful.

Dilah frowned. He'd been so happy to see his old friend that he'd forgotten to ask what on earth he was doing so far from home! "But Egg . . . what are you doing here?"

"I came searching for you," Egg said. "I decided to join you on your quest after all."

"Wow! But what about your parents? I thought you'd decided to go stay with them instead?"

The smile on Egg's face froze. "Sadly, by the time I reached home, my parents had already passed away."

"I'm so sorry . . ." Dilah reached out his paw and rested it on Egg's flipper. "What—what happened?"

"They were just old," Egg said sadly. "I was sorry not to see them one last time. I was their only family. But they were surrounded by loving friends when they died. I think after that, I realized how important friends really are." He smiled shyly at Dilah. "So, I came to find you."

Dilah smiled back. "Great! Welcome to our group! You've already met the others?"

"We've made our introductions," said Ankel.

"But how did you find us?" Dilah asked Egg.

"Remember, when you first started on your quest, I saw

which way the moonstone pointed. I've never forgotten that direction. I can't travel very quickly over land, of course, so I decided to swim around the land . . . You know, everything joins up eventually. I had a little help along the way. Sea animals are very smart. And mermaids can be helpful too . . ." Egg beamed. "The mermaid I met told me of this island—Fox Island. She thought it could be where the patron saint of white foxes hid his treasure . . . though I couldn't possibly say why . . ." he joked as he gestured up at the huge fox-shaped mountain. The rock was deepest black—volcanic, Dilah guessed—and peppered with lush tropical vegetation. "Anyway, I've been hanging out here for a while, waiting for you."

"Fox Island . . . Strange that I never heard of it before," Dilah mused. "Could this really be natural?" He gazed back up at the mountain. It really was like a large, spectacular stone statue. Dilah could clearly make out the fox's head, two pointy ears, straight nose, limbs, and tail coiled up around its huge body. It perfectly resembled a giant fox lying in the middle of the island, staring at the sea. "I guess that's where we have to go," Dilah said.

"Let's hang out for a bit here," Egg suggested. "The four of you nearly drowned! You could use some food and rest."

Egg swam into the shallow sea and showed off his fishing skills. Sometimes, he flitted across the bottom of the sea; sometimes, he leapt out of the water mischievously, stirring up a stream of crystal spray. Dilah and Ankel happily waited near shore to collect Egg's catch. A few minutes later, a pile of silvery icefish landed on the beach. Fish fresh from the sea was Dilah's favorite food. He hadn't eaten it in more than a year. Finally, he could have a good meal! Meanwhile, Little Bean, the sole herbivore, foraged for food inland and returned with a hearty harvest of greens.

They all lounged on the golden beach, munching their meals and chatting in the sun as they caught one another up on their adventures.

"Wow—you've been through more in a year and a half than Grandpa Turtle has in his whole life!" Egg exclaimed, clapping his flippers, when Dilah had finished telling him about their adventures.

An image of the greedy, cunning old turtle sunbathing on an Arctic beach flashed through Dilah's mind. He smiled fondly at the memory. He'd come so far since then!

That afternoon, as he snoozed after eating, Dilah realized the reflection in the prophet's spring had been Egg waiting in the sea. He should've figured that out earlier! And of course, Egg brought courage. Everything was coming together. Now that all five attributes of humanity had been assembled, it was time for Dilah to lead his companions toward their shared dream.

CHAPTER 10

Fox Island

The night sky unfurled its wings, and the full moon, wrapped in wisps of clouds, cast its silver light over Fox Island. Dilah solemnly opened his parcel on the beach, revealing the moonstone. The moonstone reacted differently this time: The golden crescent in the center emitted an intense glow and flickered on and off, on and off—like a heartbeat. Suddenly, with the brightest beam of light Dilah had seen emanating from the stone, it pointed toward the fox-shaped rock in the middle of the island. Just as Dilah had suspected.

They set off immediately.

The five friends were a few minutes up in the foothills, Egg pushing himself along on his belly, when Ankel glanced over his shoulder at the sea. "Look!" he hissed, and pointed to the vast moonlit bay. A small gray sailboat slowly beached on the shore, and several animals jumped off, one after another. To Dilah's surprise, Opal was the first one out of the boat. As usual, she strutted like a peacock, swishing her magnificent fluffy tail.

But Dilah's surprise turned to horror when he saw who jumped onto the beach next; his white fur shone in the moonlight as he landed gingerly on his permanently injured leg.

"Carl!" Dilah fumed as he watched several Arctic foxes and two fierce hyenas follow Carl ashore. "He's still on our tail!"

"How's that possible? How did he get here?" Ankel asked, his eyes wide in disbelief.

"Opal must've seen where we were headed," Tyrone said flatly.

Dilah felt awful. All of this was his fault! He shouldn't have trusted the cat in the first place.

"The terrain is complicated, it's a slow climb," Ankel reasoned. "We've got a head start, but"—he glanced at Egg, who was fast as a bullet in the sea but struggled on land—"our pace is a little slower. We must find the collar as quickly as possible!"

"Ankel's right. Let's hurry!" Dilah said. The group picked up their pace as much as possible.

They traveled through the night, trekking up toward the fox-shaped peak. As the sun rose, tinging the sky deep red, they neared the summit of the foothills and noticed a large lake resting in the stomach of the fox-shaped mountain, circled by the giant fox's curved legs and high back . . . and it was floating, water spilling over its edges and into clouds of vapor, just like the waterfall in the enchanted forest.

"How marvelous!" breathed Egg, his jaw dropping to the ground.

He was right. It was a magical scene, and Dilah felt his breath catch. He felt too a mysterious force urging him onward, as if a great magnet were summoning him along the path.

Dilah was about to start climbing farther when he heard a long, drawn-out cry.

"Heeeeelp!"

"Did you hear that?" Dilah asked Little Bean, who was sitting at his side. Little Bean frowned.

"Somebody help me!" the voice yelled again.

"I did that time!" said Little Bean. "Sounds like someone's in trouble."

"But who on earth could be here?" Ankel puzzled. "All day we've heard nothing but seagulls. This island doesn't seem inhabited."

"We better go have a look," Dilah replied.

The five friends sought out the source of the noise, venturing off the path.

"Ouch, it hurts!" that mysterious voice yelped again—closer yet as they walked cautiously into the lush undergrowth. "Help!"

The voice was coming from a dense bush a short distance away. They walked over and pulled back the branches. An old Arctic fox sat in the dirt. Dilah had never seen such an old fox. She had a pointed, crooked nose; a hunched back; and folds of drooping skin hanging around her neck. Nearly all her white fur was gone. Oddly, she had a pair of bloodred eyes, shining like two rubies.

"Madam, what's the matter?" Dilah asked politely.

"My stomach hurts . . . Please, help me!" The fox hunched over, clearly in pain.

"Where does it hurt? Show me." Little Bean hopped forward to examine her.

"All of it hurts!" she said.

"What about here?" Little Bean placed his front paw on the middle of her abdomen.

"Ouch! Don't be so rough—you almost killed me!" the elderly fox snapped.

"Please forgive me," Little Bean said, concerned. "I think you might've eaten something that upset your stomach. Can you think of what that might have been?"

"You don't have to treat me. I want to go home. Please take me home," the elderly fox said.

"All right, madam, but what're you doing here? Aren't you an Arctic fox?" Dilah asked.

"I could ask you the same thing." The elderly fox's eyes gleamed sharply. She might have been old, but this fox had all her wits.

"Are you also looking for the treasure?" Dilah guessed.

"I'm not interested in any treasure. I just want to go home," the elderly fox said stubbornly. "Please help me."

"Carl's still on the island. He could show up any minute. If we don't get a move on . . ." Ankel interjected anxiously.

"But we can't just leave her," Dilah objected.

"Don't talk about me as if I weren't here!" the old fox snapped. "It's rude!"

The friends were at a loss. The fox was a little grumpy to say the least, despite the fact she was asking for help. And how did she get here in the first place?

"Madam, where's home? We'll take you," Little Bean said, his voice tinged with sincerity and kindness. "If you climb on my friend's back . . ." He glanced at Tyrone pleadingly. The big panda rolled his eyes but lay down, waiting for his elderly passenger to climb on board.

Once the old fox had shakily crawled onto his fur, she curled up, coiling against his back like a withered old tree root.

"How comfortable!" she said, squinting. "Head over there!" She pointed the way to Dilah, who set off at the head of the group.

"Madam, if you don't mind me asking, how old are you?" Little Bean asked.

"Hmm, I can't remember . . . Let's see . . . Maybe a thousand or so?" the elderly fox said.

"That's impossible!" Little Bean said.

"Hmph! If you don't believe me, forget it!" The elderly fox tugged at Tyrone's ears, pointing at one of the rear legs of Fox Mountain. "No, no, no, not that way! It's this way!"

They soon came to the mountain fox's foot. They gazed up. The lake in the fox's stomach was now higher than them, floating hundreds of feet in the air. Following the old fox's directions, they went down to the lake and found a well-hidden gated archway in the near-vertical stone wall.

"All right, my good lad, put me down. I'm—I'm home . . ." the elderly fox said, gritting her teeth in pain.

Tyrone placed her on the ground. She clutched her stomach, her expression grave. Little Bean rushed over again, tending to her as gently as he could. "I think we could use a little privacy," he said to the others pointedly.

"Come look!" Ankel shouted, walking over to the stone gate. Dilah, Egg, and Tyrone followed. The arched surround of the gateway was embedded in a rough stone wall, bordered by green vines. The stone gate itself was intricately carved and had a fox relief in the center. The fox sat perfectly upright, its tail curled high, its eyes two black holes. There was a strange line of symbols underneath.

Behind them, the elderly fox crouched on the ground, trembling and groaning, and started to throw up. Little Bean gently patted her back, mumbling words of comfort. At last, her whole body shook, and the old fox spat out something slimy onto the stony ground.

"Thank you, kind rabbit. I feel much better," she croaked, slumping onto the ground in relief.

The elderly fox looked at Little Bean kindly. Then, bizarrely, her body started to smoke, the outline blurring. Panicking, Little Bean reached for her, but his paw sliced right through her body.

Before their very eyes, a living fox disappeared into thin air!

"She—she—" Little Bean stammered, gazing down at his paws as if they had been responsible.

"How . . . ?" Dilah started.

"She's gone!" Little Bean exclaimed.

Dilah, Tyrone, Ankel, and Egg ran over to look too. The elderly fox had disappeared . . . but a pool of her vomit remained. And something glittered inside it. Frowning, Dilah fished it out: a long golden key!

"What is this?" Dilah studied it closely.

The five friends brought the key over to the archway, minds brimming with questions. The stone fox's previously hollow eyes now glowed with two large rubies. *Like the old fox's eyes!* Dilah thought.

"What does that writing in Classical Animalese say above the gate?" Dilah asked Ankel.

"It says, 'Tell me your purpose,'" Ankel replied.

"Well . . . I guess we just . . ." Dilah cleared his throat. "We've come in search of the Collar of Reincarnation," Dilah proclaimed, staring at the large ruby eyes doubtfully.

Everyone jumped when a cold voice emerged from the gate. "Who sent you?" The stone fox was speaking!

"Um . . . Ulla, I guess," Dilah replied.

"Please show me your credentials," the stone fox said solemnly.

Dilah glanced at his friends doubtfully. Then he removed the parcel from around his neck and opened it in front of the ruby eyes, revealing the moonstone. Immediately, beams of blue light arced from the stone, scattering patches of blue on the gate.

"Enter," the stone fox said. "But only one animal can be tested per level. If you violate this rule, the test will end early, and you will fail."

Dilah swallowed, his throat dry. "Very well. We're ready to begin."

"The test has already begun," the stone fox said. "The

first level has been passed." The fox's eyes flashed red, and then it disappeared from the archway, leaving behind a keyhole.

"We passed the first level?" Egg said, frowning. "But how . . . ?"

"The old fox! Kindness!" Dilah leapt up excitedly, holding the gleaming key. Everyone stared at him in confusion. "Kindness was one of the human attributes Gulev said we needed to pass through the Gate of Reincarnation—so helping the sick fox must've been the first test! Little Bean, you did it!"

The rabbit flattened his ears bashfully but accepted the praise as Egg clapped him on the back and Ankel shook his paw enthusiastically.

"Now, shall I try the key?" Dilah suggested.

The keyhole was fox height, of course, so Dilah himself inserted the key and gently turned it with his mouth. As the lock clicked, the archway rumbled, the crack in the gate shaking as gravel and dust fell. The gate slowly opened, revealing a deep arched tunnel beyond.

Dilah took a breath and stepped inside.

The friends were a few paces inside when they heard the rumble of the gate closing. There was no going back now.

For a while, they continued along the passage in pitch-darkness, Dilah treading carefully at the head of the group, swishing his tail around to feel the narrow walls on either side. At one point, Little Bean lost his footing and fell with a thud. But finally, the footsteps began to echo a little more in the space around them, and the air felt different, and Dilah could tell they'd reached an open cave.

"Careful," he whispered. "Let's stay close to the wall."

Chills ran up Dilah's spine. The five friends held their breath, and Dilah swore his heart was loud enough to echo through the chamber.

"One more step, and you'll fall into the netherworld," a cold voice echoed in the cave. It was the same voice they'd heard at the gate coming from the stone fox.

Terrified, they stopped, Ankel crashing into Little Bean as they both jumped.

"Ahead of you might be an abyss, or a marsh, or a savage beast, or your natural enemy. Will the bravest among you step forward?"

Dilah felt as though there were a shotgun pointing out of the never-ending darkness, aimed right at him, the trigger ready to be pulled. The way his mother and father had died. The way Emily had died. The fears he'd buried deep in his heart gnawed at his resolve, and he felt as if a pair of invisible iron hands were gripping his neck, strangling him. His heart pounded against his chest as his trembling limbs felt glued to the ground.

"Let me go see what tricks it has up its sleeves!" Egg said, sliding himself boldly to the front of the group.

"I can feel the fear spreading inside your heart. Are you sure you want to proceed?" the voice called out.

"Why not?" Egg asked.

"Do you dare tell me what your greatest fear is?"

"Let's cut to the chase—it's fire!"

No sooner had the echoes of his voice died down than a fire broke out in front of the five friends. Dilah's eyes smarted and stung, unused to the brightness after his long walk through pitch-black, and he felt real, burning heat against his face. He glanced at Egg as his eyes adjusted. The seal's face was determined, but even so, Dilah could tell it was costing his friend enormous strength to even face up to the flames.

Dilah looked around the cave, now brilliantly lit up by the fire dancing impossibly across the smooth stone floor. The ceiling of the large square cavern was held up by four huge stone pillars, carved with mythical beasts and animals with human features. The fiery tongues licked from their feet all the way to another stone gate on the opposite side of the chamber. A narrow, nearly invisible path wound its way through the fire, snaking through the pillars and to the other side. As he peered through, Dilah noticed a carving of a fox, exactly as before, was etched into these gates too, red eyes glowing.

"If you wish to proceed, you must overcome your fear and walk across the cave," the stone fox said.

"Be careful, and go as fast as you can," Ankel told Egg.

"No problem!" Egg said, though his voice quavered slightly.

He eyed the flames in front of him, his heart racing, and Dilah knew the bottoms of his flippers would be burning from the scorching-hot ground. The flames were like gnarled demons, salivating, waiting to devour him. Summoning his courage, Egg strode into the fiery sea, which surged at him in waves.

Gritting his teeth, he bolted through the fire, moving as fast as he could as he followed the narrow path. The hot waves rushed over him one after another until he had all but disappeared into the brightness. Dilah was very afraid for his old friend. As he glimpsed Egg nearing the end of the huge hall, the flames in the cave rose up and converged into one gigantic fiery fox that charged toward the seal.

"Get down!" Dilah called out.

Egg covered his head and threw himself onto the ground, right in front of the gate. The gigantic fox-shaped flame swallowed him up, then disappeared.

Now the fiery sea was gone, only a few small flickering flames remaining on the ground. Egg glanced up, his body scorched and smoking, and staggered over to the stone gate. The gate opened, and a flashing light shone into the cavern. Then Egg fell flat on his back, greedily gulping the cool air rushing through from the space beyond.

The test was over. Dilah and his friends rushed over to Egg and checked him over.

"He's burnt and needs rest. It's very fortunate he has a thick layer of fat to protect him," Little Bean said after examining him.

"Oi," said Egg, grumbling even though he was half-delirious.

"Dilah," Little Bean continued, "I'm not sure Egg will be able to carry on just yet."

Dilah felt both proud of and sorry for his brave friend—he'd outdone himself. But the rabbit was right: He was obviously in no fit state to continue. "Can you stay here with Egg?" he asked Little Bean. "You two have passed your tests with flying colors. We'll handle the rest and come back for you, if that sounds OK?"

"That sounds sensible to me," said Little Bean, hopping over to examine more of Egg's burns. "Good luck."

Leaving Egg and Little Bean, Dilah, Ankel, and Tyrone walked through the stone gate.

The gate shut behind them with a bang. Dilah hoped Little Bean and Egg would be OK on their own.

They stood in another cave—this time arched and with two bright torches burning on either side of the entrance. A circular platform made of stone slabs stood in the center, and red murals were carved on the smooth stone walls of the cave. The space was some kind of arena. The murals looked familiar, and Dilah quickly realized they were very similar to the ones in Gulev's cave, depicting the origin of the moonstone and the birth of the Collar of Reincarnation. There was a square stone gate opposite the entrance. *It must lead to the next test*, Dilah thought.

They gingerly stepped toward the platform at the center of the arena, wondering who would be tested this time. On the way, Ankel surveyed the murals on the walls with great interest, murmuring to himself. The three friends cast elongated shadows in the center of the arena. The shadows grew longer and larger as they walked farther and farther from the fire. Gradually, as they reached the center, the huge black shadow in front of Tyrone began boiling, violently shaking, black fog rolling outward. Soon, a black-and-white face appeared. Dilah and Ankel recoiled in horror, but Tyrone's expression was different . . . His eyes brightened. The face appeared to be familiar.

Tyrone swayed. A black-and-white body with four limbs slowly crawled out of his dark shadow. The body grew thicker and denser until another panda stood on the circular stone platform. The panda was small and thin, and her eyes, surrounded by the distinctive black markings, were like two gaping holes. To Dilah, she looked like a ghost. She shook off the black mist swirling around her and tilted her head, surveying Tyrone. "Lin, is that you?" Tyrone asked softly, trembling, his gaze fixed on the female panda.

Dilah's fur stood on end as a voice emerged from the panda. It felt unreal, sharp, like fingernails scratching glass. "Tyrone?" the panda said softly.

"You—you're still alive?" Tyrone walked over to Lin. "I thought . . . Your note . . ."

"Come closer." Lin breathed deep as Tyrone stepped onto the platform, as though she were smelling something extremely tasty. Was it Dilah's imagination, or did her body grow slightly larger and firmer as she inhaled?

She stood taller, stronger, more . . . real. "Yes . . . that's better."

Meanwhile, Tyrone appeared to be diminishing as Lin was growing. It was as though a straw had been inserted into his body and his strength was being sucked out. His shoulders started to sag.

"Why did you run off, leaving only a letter?" he asked, his voice choked with tears. "You promised that we'd meet in the human world. I thought you were waiting for me there! I've spent many months following you . . . What happened?"

"I'm here now, aren't I? Don't you want to help me, Tyrone?" Lin said, smacking her lips. "Can't you see? I'm getting better by the second!" The hollowness was leaving her face, even as Tyrone started to droop further, his cheeks gaunt. "I just need you to come a little closer . . ."

"Lin, why aren't you answering me?" Tyrone burst into tears, the fat drops rolling down his face and landing on the stone slabs of the arena. "I've missed you so much. I never wanted you to go. You were my best friend, Lin. I was happy caring for you . . ."

"Enough! I'm sick of your complaints." Lin appeared to measure her new strength. Now her fur was glossy and her eyes bright. She pulled back her fist. Tyrone didn't even dodge out of the way. She hit him square on his nose. Blood dripped onto the platform, and Tyrone slumped to the floor.

"Oh no!" Ankel said, realization falling over his face. He shouted, "Tyrone, it's not her at all! It's a shadow spirit!" But it was as if the panda couldn't hear anything but Lin's voice.

"A shadow spirit?" Dilah repeated. He'd never heard of such a thing!

"An ancient spirit that lurks in cold, dark places, anywhere sunlight can't reach, waiting for its prey . . ." Ankel swallowed. "I should have thought of it right away!"

"Its prey?" Dilah asked.

"Animals," Ankel whispered as they watched Tyrone slowly push himself to his feet. "The shadow spirit creeps into an animal's shadow and learns their heart. Then, it'll trick them into fear, love, confusion . . . Through these strong emotions, it'll suck their strength and eventually suck their soul clean out of their body, so that the shadow spirit can go inside."

Dilah watched wide-eyed as the shadow spirit disguised as Lin beamed down at Tyrone, as though she'd lost all sanity. He couldn't let this dreadful creature inhabit his friend!

"Maybe I deserved that," Tyrone said. "Maybe I didn't take good enough care of you." He wiped the blood from his nose.

Lin punched him again. *Thump*. Again, Tyrone didn't try to avoid her punch. His eyes rolled in his head.

"Fight back!" Ankel and Dilah called out desperately. "It's a trick!"

"Lin, I get it. I do deserve this." He was so weak now, he was nearly a shadow himself. "If this is what it takes for you to forgive me . . ." Tyrone said, choking back sobs. "You were so brave. Now it's time for me to be brave too, isn't it?"

She punched Tyrone in the stomach with a dull thump, her fist sinking deep into his belly.

Tyrone spat out a mouthful of blood. Frowning, he

clutched his stomach and curled up on the platform, trembling with pain.

"Fight back, Tyrone!" Dilah shouted, tears in his eyes. He started forward, but Ankel put a little paw on his leg.

"The stone fox said one animal per level," he said softly, "or else . . ."

Dilah trembled with frustration.

"Lin . . ." Tyrone said, not bothering to raise himself up this time. "I knew we would be together on the other side, just like your letter said . . . but I hate that you felt you had to . . . had to leave me to die . . ."

Ankel wiped a tear from his eye. At last, Dilah pieced together the story. Lin had been terminally ill and didn't want to burden Tyrone any longer. She'd decided to leave him, writing a letter asking him to meet her in the human world, where she hoped to be reincarnated after her death.

Dilah watched with horror as his friend's white fur turned gray.

"How do we stop this?" Dilah asked Ankel. "We have to help him!"

"We have to trust him," Ankel said, clearly struggling

to keep his voice calm. "He needs to see the shadow spirit's true face. Once he does that, he'll start to fight."

Tyrone was speaking again. "Please, Lin . . . forgive me. I've kept your hat this whole time, the one you wore when you were so ill, you couldn't bear the sun in your eyes. See?" Wincing in pain, Tyrone carefully removed the battered bamboo hat from his head. "No matter what difficulties I encountered, as long as I saw it, I knew you were still by my side." Lin frowned at the tattered hat and batted it roughly away with a wave of her paw. When it hit the ground, it fell apart completely. Tyrone stared at the strips of bamboo on the ground.

Lin clenched her fists, a cold murderous air in her eyes, and swung at Tyrone yet again. Dilah's and Ankel's hearts were in their stomachs. If she hit him one more time, he might not be able to stand back up. There was a loud *thwack*—but the blow had hit Tyrone in the palm of his paw. In the blink of an eye, he'd stopped Lin's attack. The two pandas glowed in the flickering light. They stared at each other in silence, the atmosphere subtly changing.

"You're not Lin!" Tyrone said, gazing directly into the

shadow spirit's face, his eyes blazing with fury. He gripped the shadow spirit's fist and crunched hard. Dilah felt his spirits lift. At his side, Ankel cheered.

"Aren't we friends anymore?" the shadow spirit said. But her attempt at pitifulness was unconvincing even to Dilah's eyes.

"Why are you pretending to be Lin? Who or what are you?" Tyrone drew back his fist and punched.

The shadow spirit shrank, dodging the blow—and somehow, she knocked Tyrone over. The two pandas wrestled in the stone arena. The shadow spirit had the advantage of strength, but Tyrone was determined. He grasped her paws as he tried to block her punches, but he was too weak to restrain her for long. She pulled hard to release herself, and Tyrone let go. She was unbalanced by her own force and rolled to the edge of the platform. Tyrone scrambled to his feet, wiped the blood from his face, and glared down at his enemy.

She had stolen his strength, but she couldn't steal his wits.

The bears were evenly matched. As the fight continued

in a blur of fur, claws, and teeth, Dilah was on the edge of his paws.

Finally, the spirit knocked Tyrone down and grabbed him by the scruff of his neck, ready to finish the job and sap the last of his strength. His face red, Tyrone stumbled backward, tears running down his cheeks and onto the stone floor. The shadow spirit stepped on his tears as she approached him at the edge of the ring. All of a sudden, like drops of water splattering against hot coals, a cloud of smoke rose from her foot. Lifting it up, she jumped back in pain, appearing suddenly frightened.

"What's happening?" Dilah asked Ankel.

"Tyrone is overcoming his guilt and fear," Ankel said. "His tears are tears of love. And if there's one thing shadow spirits hate, it's love."

Tyrone rose to his feet. Now the shadow spirit was edging backward.

"You're not Lin—you don't even look like her!" Tyrone seized the opportunity to rush over and attack the shadow spirit's face with all his might.

Crash. The shadow spirit's face cracked like a porcelain

jar. Black smoke streamed out of the broken face like ink, flowing beneath Tyrone's body, reassembling into his shadow, until the spirit was no more.

The square stone door opened. Tyrone slumped to the ground, exhausted, wheezing.

"Are you OK?" Dilah and Ankel hurried to Tyrone's side. "You were amazing!"

"Don't worry about me," Tyrone puffed. Except for his injuries, he was clearly fully recovered from the shadow spirit's draining spell—his fur now bright white and deep black, his face round and healthy. "I can't go on right now . . . but I'll be fine after I rest! Quick, get in there. I'm counting on you!"

"Go and find Little Bean and Egg, OK?" Ankel said anxiously.

"We've got this!" Dilah said.

After a last farewell, he and Ankel walked through the next stone door.

The cave beyond was square, this time with numerous torches lining the walls, fully lighting up the inside. In the middle of the cave stood an enormous hourglass: three gold pillars supporting two connected crystal balls, the bottom one filled with fine white sand.

On either side of the hourglass, open stone books had been etched into the walls, a line of text engraved on each opened page. Dilah read one of the inscriptions:

... THE TWENTY-SIXTH TO BE NAMED SECOND ELDER, THE ARROGANT AND WEAK GEOFFREY, LATER LOUIS I.

He then peered at another stone book:

... THE NINETY-THIRD TO BE NAMED PATRIARCH, THE ROMANTIC AND ARTISTIC TELEMANN, LATER CHARLES III.

Who were these people, and what did these inscriptions mean?

Meanwhile, Ankel studied a stone book that was engraved with the inscription:

... THE HUNDREDTH TO BE NAMED FOURTH ELDER, THE BRILLIANT GENIUS WILLIAM, LATER NAPOLEON BONAPARTE.

"Who's that?" Dilah asked his friend.

"I remember Grandfather mentioning the name *Napoleon*. He was someone very famous in the human world, long ago."

"A human!" Dilah glanced at Ankel. "Do you think these are the names of foxes who went through the Gate of Reincarnation and the humans they transformed into?" he suggested.

"Could be . . ." Ankel said. "But where's the challenge?"

Dilah gazed around the room. Once again, on the wall opposite them, was a closed double door, but a book made of pure gold was inlaid between these two doors, rather than the usual fox. As he drew closer, Dilah noticed that in the middle of the open page sat a little golden fox with familiar ruby eyes.

"Look at this," Dilah said to Ankel. "There's an inscription in the door too. It's for Nicholas."

THE HUNDRED AND THIRTY-FOURTH TO BE NAMED PATRIARCH, THE TALENTED LEADER OF THE ARCTIC FOXES NICHOLAS, LATER LEONARDO, THE SON OF A FOREST WATCHMAN.

Leonardo . . . Where had Dilah heard that name before? He shook his head—he couldn't place it.

"Hang on . . ." said Ankel, his eyes widening. "Son of a forest watchman . . . Couldn't that be—"

Just then, the little golden fox on the open pages sprang to life, blinking its ruby eyes. "We meet again, Dilah," he called out in his familiar, cold voice. "Though I haven't properly introduced myself. I am the Collar of Reincarnation."

Dilah and Ankel blinked in shock. How could the collar be a series of little stone foxes and not a collar at all? And how could it talk?

"Are you ready for your next test?" the golden fox asked.

Dilah nodded. "We're ready."

"Good. To pass through these doors, you must answer

my three questions before the hourglass is finished. You must answer all three correctly in order to advance to the next level," the little golden fox explained. "Have you decided which of you is going to answer the questions?"

Dilah glanced at his friend. Ankel took a deep breath and confidently walked over to the hourglass. "Let the questions begin!"

"Very good. Now, answer me this. A weasel spends days foraging for food, storing the uneaten food in his burrow for his old age. The stored food is enough for a dozen weasels to enjoy for a lifetime. However, when the weasel finally retires to his burrow, he ends up starving to death. Why?"

As soon as the fox's voice ceased, the huge hourglass spun over and began its countdown, the sands in the upper ball flowing to the lower. Dilah glanced at his friend nervously, but he was reassured by the confident smile on Ankel's face.

"Because the weasel neglected to store any rocks on which to grind his teeth. As a result, his front teeth continue to grow, and he's unable to chew."

"Correct," the golden fox said mechanically, its two ruby eyes glowing red.

Swoosh! To Dilah's amazement, the sand at the bottom of the hourglass magically flew back upward.

"The second one is a riddle." The little fox then recited:

What is sometimes fast, sometimes slow,
Makes no noise, and leaves no trace?
Hides beneath hills, yet can wear them away,
Hides behind stars, but can make them grow faint?
Can swallow everything whole, can make everything change,
Arrives filled with hope, often leaves behind heartache?

The sands in the hourglass began sifting down again, rustling as they fell. Dilah sat down, trying to figure out the answer for himself. *What is sometimes fast, sometimes slow . . . ? The wind? No, the wind makes noise! Can swallow everything whole, can make everything change . . . The night? No, the night couldn't wear away the hills.* He had a hunch that the answer must be very different from anything he was thinking. He glanced anxiously over at Ankel.

"It's time!" the weasel answered a moment later. "Time always passes quickly when we're happy, and slowly when we're in pain. It comes filled with hope, but slips away, leaving heartache."

The little golden fox was silent, as if stunned at the speed with which Ankel had figured out the answer. Its ruby eyes flashed, and the sands flew back.

"Correct," it said. "And the third and final question. Three animals are sitting around an apple: a fox, a weasel, and a rabbit. Red and blue butterflies are fluttering about. One lands on each animal's head. They can't see the butterfly on their own head and can only see the butterflies on the other animals' heads. Everyone wants to eat the apple, but only one of them may have it. For the sake of fairness, the three animals have negotiated two rules: If one of them sees that the other two animals have red butterflies on their heads, then they can eat the apple; if one knows that a blue butterfly is on their own head, then they can eat the apple. Let's say you're the weasel, and you see blue butterflies on the heads of the fox and rabbit. After a long while, no one has touched the apple. What color is the butterfly on your head?"

The hourglass started all over again. After hearing the question, Dilah's mind went totally blank. He watched the white grains of sand quickly flow down, his heart racing. Ankel ignored the hourglass and sat on the ground, deep in thought. He picked up three pebbles and arranged them into a triangle. He placed his small paw over his mouth and began chewing on the claw on his forefinger, while his other paw moved around the three stones as he mumbled to himself.

After a while, he lifted his hand and calmly shouted, "Blue!"

"Why?" asked the little golden fox, its voice tinged with surprise.

"The butterfly on my head can only be red or blue. If it's red, the fox will see a blue butterfly on the rabbit's head and the red butterfly on my head. If the fox also has a red butterfly on their head, then the rabbit will see two red butterflies and eat the apple immediately. But the rabbit doesn't eat it, so the fox will assume that they have a blue butterfly on their head, which means, according to the rules, they could eat the apple. But the fox doesn't eat it either, so the hypothesis that I have a red butterfly on my head doesn't hold up. Thus, I also must have a blue butterfly on my head!" Ankel answered, keeping cool and composed.

"Correct," the little golden fox said admiringly. "You didn't even use half the time. You're the smartest animal I've ever met!"

"Thank you!" Ankel said gleefully, pleased to earn the praise of the Collar of Reincarnation.

"He's right, Ankel—that was incredible." Dilah was finally able to release the tension in his body.

"Thanks, Dilah," the weasel replied cheerfully.

Dilah's admiration for Ankel grew. How had his friend's little brain been able to solve the puzzles so quickly?! Amazing!

"Congratulations on passing all of my tests!" the little golden fox said. "I am willing to accept Dilah as my master. However, the last attribute has a different kind of test. If you pass, then I'm yours. Go in! The white fox Anubis is waiting for you inside!" The little golden fox's red eyes flashed, and then it disappeared from the golden book. The book closed, and the two stone doors thundered open.

Anubis. Dilah shivered, remembering his vision of the nine tails in the spring and Gulev's grim warning. He turned to Ankel.

"Ankel, you should go back, look after Tyrone, and find the others. I have to face this alone. Just know that being your friend has been the greatest honor of my life!" Dilah said.

"Likewise, Dilah," Ankel said gently. He reached out and hugged the white fox tightly. "You're going to be just fine," he whispered in Dilah's ear.

Dilah pulled away gently. If he didn't go now, he thought he might cry. Gulping down his tears, he walked through the stone doors.

Dilah entered a cold, damp cave filled with bright blue light that reminded him of an Arctic ice cave in the sunlight. He glanced over his shoulder as the doors shut, glimpsing Ankel's little face watching him before they closed completely, leaving Dilah truly alone.

One last test. Everything had been leading to this. He walked on.

Stalactites hung from the roof of the cave. Some were like sharp ice swords pointed over Dilah's body, dripping with crystal clear water that hit pools on the ground with crystalline clicks. Others were like frozen waterfalls, and some were connected to the stalagmites on the ground, forming towering blue columns.

Dilah walked toward the center of the cave, his paws splashing lightly in the shimmering puddles on the cave floor. At the center, a stone fox surrounded by half-frozen blue ripples sat perched atop a cone-shaped stone platform, peering down as if in disapproval. Nine long tails held up the large crystal-like ceiling like nine stone pillars. Or . . . *was* it crystal? Dilah lifted his eyes. The ceiling, he realized, was *water*. He was under the floating blue lake in the belly of Fox Mountain! Blue ribbons of sunlight swirled through from outside, fish flitting to and fro overhead like strange silver birds.

Dilah approached the nine-tailed fox statue. The stone platform was engraved with strange symbols and patterns and adorned with fox totem decorations. Two foxes were carved in the middle of the platform, sitting back-to-back with curled-up tails. Between the arch of their tails was the poem that was so familiar to Dilah:

I was formed in the Arctic.
I bring hope and guide the way.
I'm filled with sky and moon,
on behalf of the northern night . . .

Dilah lifted his gaze to meet the stern, piercing eyes of the nine-tailed fox. And that's when he noticed a glittering object around the statue's neck. His eyes widened—it was a collar!

The Collar of Reincarnation.

Dilah drew closer, keeping to the frozen parts of the pool surrounding the statue, and examined the golden, glowing collar with bated breath. In the middle of the collar, the familiar little golden fox with ruby eyes held up a large pale blue gemstone with its head and curved tail.

A small golden crescent was imprinted in the middle of the gem—it had to be the other part of the moonstone! Five smaller foxes were carved beneath the red-eyed fox, each in a different lifelike pose, joined from head to tail around the circumference of the collar. Each little fox was engraved with a word in Classical Animalese. Dilah couldn't read the ancient language but guessed the words were *faith*, *wisdom*, *kindness*, *courage*, and *love*.

"Who's there?" a gravelly voice rumbled from the statue. Dilah nearly jumped out of his skin.

"Um . . . I'm Dilah," he replied.

"My name is Anubis," the nine-tailed fox said. Stone creaked and clicked as his mouth sprang to life, his eyes shifting. Finally, his gaze settled on Dilah. But the rest of his body remained stony and immovable.

"You're young . . . but you're larger than the average Arctic fox," Anubis observed.

"I drank from the spring of the enchanted forest," Dilah replied.

"If you were able to enter the enchanted forest, you must have extraordinary abilities," Anubis mused, an impressed expression flitting across his face in a ripple of white.

But Dilah shrugged. "I was just lucky."

"If that's the case, then how did you pass the other tests?"

"My friends helped me," Dilah explained.

"Oh? How many foxes are there?" Anubis asked.

"There aren't any other foxes. There's a seal, a weasel, a rabbit, and a panda."

"Different species? You're working with other species?" A chilly tone had entered Anubis's voice. "You let them in on the greatest secret of the Arctic foxes? You disappoint me!"

Dilah urged himself to stay calm, remembering Gulev's advice. "They're friends I made along the way. We share the same dream."

"You're not worthy of the collar," Anubis barked. "Get out!"

Dilah stayed where he was.

"Oh, you won't go? Clueless little boy . . ."

Dilah heard the sound of ice breaking overhead.

Looking up, he saw a thick stalactite falling toward him! Startled, he jumped out of the way.

Boom!

The stalactite snapped in a shallow pool of water, which splashed all over him. But still, he held his ground.

"You still won't go?" Anubis said, as though he was warning him. Three stalactites trembled threateningly over Dilah's head.

"I can't go. Everyone's counting on me!"

The three stalactites dropped, one after the other. Dilah darted left and right. Two of the sharp pillars brushed past him, and the last one grazed his chest, knocking him into the pool. He felt a sharp pain but pulled his body out of the water, staggering to his feet.

"If you give up now, I'll let you out," Anubis said sternly. "For the last time, are you going?"

The whole cave appeared to tremble now. The stalactites and stalagmites creaked and crackled, pointing unnaturally toward Dilah. There was nowhere to hide.

"I'm not going! I'll never give up my dream!" Dilah shouted at the top of his lungs, his eyes glinting with determination, drops of blood trickling down his fur and whirling in the water.

There was a moment of silence.

"You're really not afraid of death," Anubis said, his tone softening. The cave stopped trembling. The horrifying creaking and cracking noises ceased as the pillars of sharp ice returned to their natural positions. Dilah let out a slow, thin breath of relief. "I see the fire of determination burning in your heart," Anubis continued. "Tell me— what will you do if you don't get this treasure?"

"I'll bless its master, then find another way."

"You have integrity. Perhaps this is the difference between me and you . . . My old heart is full of selfishness and evil thoughts, so I ended up like this," Anubis said in a low voice. He looked like an ice sculpture in the blue light.

"Can you tell me your story?" Dilah asked.

"I'm ashamed to talk about my ugly past," Anubis sighed softly. "Centuries ago, I was the first to guard the Collar of Reincarnation. But after watching countless adventurers ascend to the human realm, I started to wish I could follow. I killed the next white fox who came in search of the treasure and ran off with the collar myself."

A bubbling sound from the ceiling broke the silence in the cave. The shadow of a fish swam across Anubis's face.

"But I was caught before I could use it, and Ulla was furious. He gave me eight more tails as a punishment. Each tail represents one life. This means that if I want to become a human being, I have to use the collar nine times, dying nine deaths. I begged Ulla for forgiveness. Instead, Ulla asked me to guard the collar for life. To prevent me from making the same mistake I had made before, he turned me into a stone statue and has kept me prisoner here ever since, doomed to continue watching other foxes achieve what I never can . . . I've been living in regret ever since. To lose the trust of the saint is to lose the meaning of existence."

"You're wrong. It's not that Ulla doesn't trust you," Dilah stated.

Anubis blinked. "What do you mean?"

"If he didn't trust you, he wouldn't let you guard the collar, would he?" Dilah said warmly. "Just because you did a bad thing once, it doesn't mean you're not worthy of forgiveness. I think Ulla forgave you long ago."

Thump-thump, thump-thump, thump-thump.

Dilah gazed at the nine-tailed statue, confused. What was that sound? Could it be . . . a heartbeat?

As Dilah watched, the center of Anubis's chest glowed silver, a circle spreading from the heart outward. As the halo widened and spread, the stone left in its wake turned to flesh and blood.

Anubis was coming back to life!

At last, the silver halo spread over the statue's neck and head. Anubis sucked in a deep breath of air and twisted his neck slightly, cracking his bones with a snap.

The nine-tailed fox started to tremble and gasped to life, before sagging onto his plinth as if exhausted. Then a magical melody sounded in the air. Dilah's eyes widened. The five little foxes on the reincarnation collar around Anubis's neck had started chanting in unison, a dignified and sacred quintet:

After years of slumber, we awaken once more.

Treasure-hunting fox, please listen carefully to our chant.

Each patron saint has a unique way to turn animals into humans,

and Ulla is no exception.

However, each patron saint has a different understanding of humans,

and values different attributes.

Thus, there are all kinds of people in the world.

Ulla said that to become human, you must possess the five virtues.

The five little foxes then spoke in turn:

"My name is Faith, the flame of hope blazing in people's hearts."

"My name is Wisdom. Without me, what difference is there between man and beast?"

"My name is Kindness. People need compassionate hearts."

"My name is Courage. I can help you obtain what you seek."

"My name is Love, the soul of all humans."

Together, they continued:

You need all five of us to pass through the Gate of
Reincarnation.
Look, the wheel of fate has quietly turned, reaching out to
greet the new dawn!
Some things, born out of love, will also die for love . . .

After they finished the last line, the music stopped, and
the five foxes on the collar grew silent and still.

"Thank you, Dilah. Of all the foxes who have come
here over the years seeking this treasure, you are the only
one to ask me my story, to show me compassion and give
me hope. You broke the spell." Anubis smiled warmly,
waving his nine bushy tails. "I promise to do three things
to repay you. But first . . ."

Dilah blinked as Anubis tucked in his ears, lowered his
neck, and slid off the Collar of Reincarnation.

Dilah stared at the gleaming gold collar, his eyes
stinging with tears, his emotions mixed. In front of him

was this treasure, exquisite beyond compare, the sum of countless hardships. This treasure that he'd risked his life for, numerous times, was nearly in his possession. Accompanied by friends, he'd crossed mountains and rivers; braved snowstorms and sea storms; endured hunger and illness; been tracked, tricked, and hunted; lost friends to death. So many times he'd been in danger, only narrowly escaping . . . Dilah blinked, two big tears flowing out. At last, his dream was coming true!

The collar didn't fall to the ground when it slipped from Anubis's neck. Instead, it floated, flipped in the air, then fastened itself around Dilah's neck. As the collar touched his body, Dilah felt his fur stand on end.

A hazy milk-white figure appeared at Dilah's side, wearing a hood and cloak. The familiar figure slowly turned to face him. The moment their eyes met, Dilah almost cried out. A fox-like human dressed in a long white robe stood before him. He had a human face, a fox's pointed noise, tufts of white fur covering his skin, and two ears sticking up in his hood. This half human, half beast was none other than the supreme patron saint of the Arctic, whom Dilah had once glimpsed in a dream.

"Ulla . . ." Dilah breathed.

"Dilah, we meet again." The ethereal voice drifted into Dilah's ears. Ulla hadn't opened his mouth—the voice emanated from everywhere and nowhere at all.

"Great patron saint, thank you for your guidance!" Dilah said in awe, bowing down to Ulla.

"You should thank yourself. Congratulations, my son, on your success . . ." Ulla's voice rang out again. The hazy figure stepped toward Dilah, his entire body emitting a soft light. "You're about to realize your dream of becoming a human being."

"But none of this came easily," Dilah said, various emotions welling up in his heart.

"Only by traveling through darkness can we reach the other side of our dreams," Ulla gently said.

"Patron Saint Ulla, may I share the reincarnation collar with my friends?"

"Of course. It already belongs to you—you can decide how to use it."

Dilah felt his heart glow.

Ulla lifted his furry hands and held them gracefully in the air. A sacred light enveloped the cave. "Are you ready, Dilah?"

"Ready!"

"Wonderful! I'll see you soon . . ."

The corners of Ulla's mouth turned up slightly as the milk-white figure, half-hidden, half-visible, gradually dissipated like mist.

As Ulla disappeared, the cave started to shake violently, stones and ice tumbling down, and a loud rumbling filled the air. Dilah glanced up. Unsupported by Anubis's nine stone tails, the crystal ceiling was cracking—breaking under the pressure of the water. Anubis too glanced up with fear in his eyes as water started to surge through the cracks. The cave was about to collapse!

"Run!" Anubis shouted, nimbly turning his body until his nine living tails supported the ceiling once more—but flesh and blood were no substitute for stone.

"But what will you do?" Dilah asked, panicking. The cracks in the crystal were spreading.

"I'll be fine! Tell the collar to close the doors after you!" Anubis shouted.

Dilah ran. Behind him, the crystal started to bow under the immense pressure of the water. Anubis's nine tails trembled and curved under the weight. The ceiling caved in halfway, the water rushing with great speed.

At the door, Dilah realized with panic that the moonstone wasn't around his neck! It must have been displaced by the collar. He glanced over his shoulder, but there was no way he could retrieve it now. He leapt through the doors and shouted at the collar, "Close the doors!"

The doors slammed shut, cutting off the torrent of water—for now.

"You've done a fine job, Dilah," the golden fox on the collar said, its voice chiming in Dilah's ears. "Congratulations on becoming my eighty-seventh master. You will have power over me for three days."

"The doors won't hold the water back forever," Dilah said anxiously. "I have to find my friends!"

Dilah bounded back the way he'd come, the doors opening each time under his command and closing again behind him, but the next two caves were empty. Finally, as the doors to the first cave they'd entered boomed open, he found his friends clustered around the remnants of the magical fire that had been Egg's test of courage.

"Dilah!" Ankel cried out delightedly, catching sight of the collar. "You did it!"

"Let's see!" said Egg excitedly, clapping his flippers.

Dilah felt relieved and overjoyed to find his friends safe and recovering—and the rumble of the lake water gushing through the ceiling of the last cave had long faded. They were safe—for now. He bounded over to Egg. Egg removed the collar from Dilah's neck and touched it to the tip of his nose.

"Ouch! It shocked me!" Egg said delightedly.

"Let me try!" Little Bean straightened his neck. Dilah lifted the collar over his head and slid it down over his plump belly. Little Bean giggled, revealing his two large front teeth.

"My turn!" Ankel said, holding out his paws in respect. Dilah removed the collar from Little Bean and placed it in Ankel's small hands. He shuddered as though he'd been electrocuted and admired the exquisite treasure with great curiosity, reading the inscriptions and examining the five fox figures. Smiling, he handed it back to Dilah.

Lastly, Dilah tossed the collar to Tyrone, who reached out and caught it. He tried to fit the collar around his neck, but his head was too big. Instead, it sat on his head as if he were wearing a golden crown. Tyrone smiled and handed the collar back to Dilah.

"Now that you've all seen it, we should go," Dilah said. "Our dream is about to come true!"

CHAPTER 11

The Reincarnation

When the five friends stepped out into the daylight, it was as though they had stepped into another world: The glare of the sun, the fresh scent of grass, and the huge blue sky all felt brilliantly new.

Dilah felt a pang of sadness, though, as he realized what had to happen next. In the next three days, he and every one of his beloved friends would have to die in order to achieve their dreams. And the collar . . . Like Nicholas,

Dilah knew he had to try to destroy it in the process.

The stone gate closed behind them with a loud rumble. The Collar of Reincarnation around Dilah's neck glittered in the sun. But when he caught sight of the boat moored on the shore, he remembered his unfinished business.

"Carl's still on the island. He'll be after us and the collar," Dilah said. "We have to destroy it before he steals it for himself."

"Destroy it?" Ankel said softly. "Are you sure this is what you want? Nicholas—"

"Nicholas was right. The collar has caused so much pain and heartbreak. I think we five should be the last ever to use it," Dilah said solemnly.

"So, what do we do?" asked Egg.

Dilah was grateful for his friends' silent, unquestioning support. He glanced up at the top of the mountain, the fox's head. "Up there. If we cast it down from such a height, it can't survive. If it does, the sea will wash it away."

"I'm in!" Tyrone agreed.

"Me too," Little Bean said, hopping.

"Carl will try to stop us," Dilah said, "if he finds us."

"I almost lost myself back there. I could use a good fight to stretch my muscles!" Tyrone said.

"Thank you, friends!" Dilah said, moved.

"We should start up the fox's tail," Ankel suggested, tracing their route with his eyes.

———◇———

A few hours later, panting, the five had climbed up the tail and reached the back of Fox Mountain. The terrain was steep on either side of the fox's rocky spine—one wrong step, and they'd be toast!

"Dilah, look!"

Dilah glanced in the direction where Ankel was pointing and gasped. Two men were using ropes to climb up the mountain, guns slung over their backs.

"Mate, do you really think there's hidden treasure here?" the shorter of the two asked, uncertain, panting as he squatted on a rock.

"Of course! There've been rumors for years, but no one's found it yet. If we get our hands on it, we'll be set for life!" the taller man said, leaning against a rock.

"I'm a firm believer in luck! This island is secluded, and the surrounding sea is stormy. Plus, we found a shortcut up the mountain. At this rate, we're guaranteed to be the first to find the treasure!"

"Darn right!" the taller man said, spitting. "Whoever the fools are who brought that other boat, they must be climbing up the other side. We'll beat them to the treasure, then take off in the boats and leave them to hang out with the seagulls in this blasted place!" He grinned wickedly.

"There are others too?" Dilah whispered uncertainly. He peered down at the bay. As they'd been walking, a larger ship had anchored farther out. The two men must have come from that, as a smaller boat had been pulled up on the shore next to the one Carl had arrived on. How hadn't they noticed before? "There's nothing we can do except get to the top before they do," Dilah said nervously. "We have to hurry! This can't fall into the hands of humans."

The friends were about to resume their climb when

Dilah caught a whiff of foxy scent. He tensed, but it was too late. While they'd been distracted by the humans, Carl had beaten them at their own game. He stalked out from behind a huge boulder, accompanied by Blake and Warren—his two hired hyenas, four Arctic foxes, and Opal the cat. The group blocked their path. Eight against five, Dilah thought nervously—and three of his group would be close to useless in a fight.

"Dilah, at last. I've been waiting for a long time to meet you again," Carl said gravely.

Dilah let out a low, rumbling growl.

"Why so sullen, little fox? We had such a hard time finding you. I set off from the Arctic with thirty strong foxes, and now only four are left . . . But thanks to the help of this cat, here we are. I hope it's worth it."

"You think I'm afraid?" Dilah walked toward Carl. "I'm not. Plus, I'm younger, bigger, and stronger than you. I could defeat you easily."

"But can your friends defeat mine?" Carl said with a slow smile, gesturing at his hyenas and foxes. Then his eyes caught on Dilah's neck. "Wait—what happened to the moonstone?" Carl asked. His eyes widened. "Could that be . . . Ulla's secret treasure?"

"Correct," Dilah said. There wasn't much point pretending otherwise.

"That's it?" The hyena Blake stared greedily at the collar, as though he were imagining himself the king of all animals.

"Though I didn't get the moonstone, this is even better. I should thank you for helping me find the treasure!" Carl said excitedly, his eyes glued to the collar.

"You're not its master," Dilah said icily. "I am."

Carl's gaze grew cold. "Don't talk to me like your father did!" he hissed. "Look what happened to him! I'll send you to the netherworld to meet him."

"I'm afraid it won't be that easy," a familiar voice called out. Another Arctic fox approached them, followed by two red foxes.

"Alsace? What're you doing here?" Carl gasped.

Dilah felt his heart lurch at the sight of his older brother, his emotions mixed. Last time he'd seen Alsace, the fox had stolen the moonstone and imprisoned him and his friends, before sending Emily along with their party as a spy. And yet, he was no friend of Carl's.

"I've been following you. When you headed out to sea, we stowed away on a ship headed to Fox Island to hunt for treasure," Alsace said, his voice as cool and collected as always. His eyes settled on Dilah's party. "Where is Emily?"

"She—she's—" Dilah stammered, lowering his eyes. Alsace understood, bowing his head but displaying no other signs of emotion.

"And . . . did you find Ulla's treasure?" Alsace asked.

Dilah puffed out his chest. "Here it is!" Dilah said excitedly. He decided to appeal to Alsace's better nature. "But, brother, I need your help. This collar is cursed. Because of it, our parents, Nicholas, Gray, and Jens are all dead—and countless others before, all chasing after the dream of transforming into humans! This treasure can no longer stay in this world, let alone end up in Carl's clutches, or even worse, the hands of humans. You have to help me destroy it."

"That's hilarious!" They turned toward the bell-like laughter. Opal licked her paw and dragged it disdainfully over her ears. "I thought this was supposed to be some

— 261 —

kind of amazing treasure, considering how you all are willing to fight to the death over it, and *this* is all it turns out to be? Who would want to become human? They're all horrible, anyway!"

"Carl, answer me—is this true?" Warren snarled. "Is it cursed?"

"You owe us an explanation!" Blake shouted. "Did all those foxes really die because of it?"

"Don't fall for his lies. This fox is trying to undermine our alliance and cheat his brother!" Carl said, narrowing his eyes. "Transforming you into a human is only one of the collar's many magic powers. Whoever has it can become the king of all animals and live forever! And there's no such thing as the curse."

"I won't let him steal the Collar of Reincarnation," Alsace said, walking over to stand by Dilah's side.

"What?" Dilah couldn't believe his ears. How could this brother who trusted him be the same as the ruthless ruler who had imprisoned him months before?

Alsace spoke as if he'd guessed at Dilah's consternation. "When I first met you, I just wanted to learn the secret of the moonstone. And I was frustrated our parents had chosen to gift the treasure to you, the younger and weaker brother. But now, seeing how strong you've become, how many tests you've had to face to get where you are, I'm happy for you. I finally understand why our parents gave the moonstone to you," Alsace said, gazing at his brother with real pride in his eyes.

Dilah felt warmth rush through his body. For the first time, Alsace truly felt like family to him.

"Did I mishear you just now? Are you saying that you, your two tired foxes, and Dilah are going up against me, Blake, Warren, and my five followers?" Carl asked with a sly smile. "I don't like your odds."

"Count me in too!" Tyrone growled.

"Ankel, Little Bean, and Egg—go hide! Quickly!" Dilah ordered.

"But—"

"No buts. You need to stay safe!"

The two sides assumed their positions, ready for a showdown. Dilah's heart raced—a fierce battle was about to break out.

The sun was sinking, casting a dazzling glow over Fox Mountain. Dilah stood on a high stone formation, cloaked in a robe of sunlight, his white coat blazing like a flame. He glowered at Carl, his teeth clenched, new and old hatred surging in his heart. This was his chance to avenge his parents.

"Let's finish this once and for all!" Dilah said, lunging at Carl. At the same time, Tyrone charged at Warren and Blake, and Alsace and his two red foxes took on the four Arctic foxes. Little Bean took Egg to hide behind a rock while Ankel climbed onto a taller rock to watch the action unfold.

Dilah was stronger than the last time he'd fought Carl—and bigger too, thanks to the stream in the enchanted forest. After his long journey, he had muscles of steel and was not the least bit afraid of the mortal enemy who'd once frightened him. He charged repeatedly at Carl, delivering smooth, clean blows. But Carl was a practiced fighter—he kept leaping from side to side, dodging Dilah's attacks despite his crooked leg.

Meanwhile, Tyrone and the hyenas were locked in a

stalemate. Whenever Tyrone landed a blow, it would have been enough to break the creatures' bones, but Blake nimbly darted left and right, draining the panda's strength, while wily Warren lurked back, searching for a weakness in the panda's defenses.

On the other side, it was Alsace versus two of the white foxes, and the two red foxes versus the other two white foxes.

Then . . . "Humans!" Ankel cried out in alarm.

Not now! Dilah thought in frustration.

Four human arms appeared over the edge of the cliff. The two treasure hunters Dilah and his friends had spotted before pulled themselves up. The taller man stood up and curiously eyed the frozen battlefield.

"A panda, Arctic foxes, a weasel, hyenas . . ." he exclaimed, scanning his surroundings. "And some of these beasts are huge! Is this a rare wildlife party?"

"Check out that fox's chest! Gold and precious stones!" the shorter man yelled.

"I told you this trip would be worth it." The taller man smiled a slow, hungry smile. He spat at his feet, then raised his gun and aimed it straight at Dilah. No time to be afraid—Dilah turned and rolled out of the way, hitting his head against a rock. *Bang.* The bullet missed him, throwing up a cloud of dust as it buried itself into the earth.

"Lousy shot. Watch this!" the shorter man sneered, raising his shotgun and aiming it at Dilah with one eye closed. Dilah's eyes widened as he struggled, dazed, to get to his feet, but the man's shot went wild, hitting a rock in the distance, splitting it into pieces of rubble. Furious, he glanced down and noticed a gray rabbit looking at him timidly with huge watery eyes.

Little Bean had whacked him in the kneecap! The man's face twisted in anger as his friend taunted him. "Stupid thing," he said, aiming his gun down.

Dilah staggered to his feet, regaining his balance. He opened his mouth to call out a warning to the brave rabbit, but it was too late.

Bang.

Little Bean's large eyes froze, his gaze blank as he fell down, and then he lay still.

"No!" Ankel cried, jumping down from his rock.

Tyrone let out a wordless roar and charged at the two humans. The two men turned white with fear and bolted. Tyrone ran over to Little Bean and lifted him in his arms, tears running down his cheeks, not realizing the short man had turned and readied his gun.

Bang.

"No!" Dilah shouted again. Tyrone's body convulsed, but he steadied himself; the shot had hit him in the shoulder. The man beamed, his gun smoking. Tyrone gently placed Little Bean on the ground and then dashed for the man. The smile dropped from the treasure hunter's face as he turned and fled in panic. Too slow. Tyrone snatched him up and threw him through the air.

Crack.

The short man smacked into a rock and fell motionless to the ground.

Bang bang.

The taller man had shot Tyrone in the back and side. Silently, Tyrone turned around and glared at him with vicious rage. The man ran. Tyrone took a few steps after him, but then he swayed, fell flat on his back, his wounds bleeding heavily.

Dilah's world was spinning. Two of his friends, dead in the space of seconds.

Soon to be reborn, he told himself firmly, fighting back his tears.

Dilah glanced at Carl, then lunged at him, teeth bared, as the battle roared back to life. In a flash, Carl leapt up to the nearest rock, then used his three good paws to springboard into the air, targeting Dilah's throat, his attack sharp and fierce. Dilah ducked out of the way, Carl soaring over him. Dilah rolled under Carl and kicked him hard in the stomach. Losing his balance, Carl toppled to the ground. Dilah seized the opportunity to pounce on Carl and pin him down. He gathered all his grief and rage and anger into strength, glaring at the older fox. *Do it. Now.* He sunk his teeth into Carl's neck without hesitation. He tasted blood. Carl closed his eyes and stopped breathing. Dilah staggered away, his elation fading into horror at what he was capable of.

"Dilah, look out—behind you!" Ankel called out.

Something struck Dilah hard and knocked him to the ground beside Carl's body. A big rock had hit him squarely on the back! He rolled over, groaning. A white puffball stood on a boulder behind him—Opal. She stared at him with her huge amber eyes narrowed into slits, grinning wickedly. Dilah tried to stagger to his feet, but Blake pounced on him, the muscular hyena pushing him to the ground.

"Did you kill Carl? Great. Now I don't have to worry about that fox stealing my treasure!" Blake said, holding Dilah down. "You poor devil. You look just like your brother did before he died," Blake said with a cruel laugh.

"Alsace?" Dilah's blood ran cold. He turned his head painfully. Sure enough, Alsace was lying in a puddle of blood nearby. Two red foxes and two Arctic foxes were also lying on the ground, lifeless or mortally wounded. Alsace's and Carl's followers. Dilah saw a hyena's body a few paces away too. "You mean, after he killed your friend?" Dilah shot back at the hyena on his chest. His anger exploded like a bomb again, his rage transforming into power. In a surge of strength, he rolled over and pushed Blake away. This worthless hyena had killed Dilah's brother, the one surviving member of his family!

Blake fell back several steps, a glint of fear in his eyes. Dilah charged at him and knocked him over. Before he could recover, Dilah struck savagely at the hyena's throat, closing his eyes and tearing hard. Blake opened his mouth wide and groaned a few times, then stopped moving. Dilah gasped and released his grip.

Suddenly, Dilah sensed a shadow moving above him. Something fell from high above and wrapped itself around his head. Opal!

"Where's the moonstone?" she screeched. "I need it! You promised you'd give it to me!"

Dilah tried to shake her off, but she clung on tight.

"Let him go, you evil cat!" There was a dull thud, and Dilah was released. He lifted his head in time to see Opal flying through the air, her fur ruffling in the breeze and a shrill scream falling from her lips as she plunged over the edge of the cliff. Egg stood in front of him, chest heaving with the effort of tearing the cat off Dilah's back.

The Collar of Reincarnation! Dilah no longer felt its weight around his neck. He looked around frantically and spotted it on a rock nearby. He dashed over to grab it, and a flash of white whizzed by as his teeth closed against the hard metal. Carl clenched the other half of the collar. The wound on his neck was bloody but shallow, and Dilah realized the wily fox had played dead!

Carl and Dilah tugged at the collar, growling.

Carl's eyes were bloodshot, and the sharp points on the collar cut his mouth. Dilah clamped down hard and pulled with all his might. The collar was loosed from Carl's grip! Dilah tossed it toward the sky before Carl could gather his strength for a second attempt. It flipped through the air, flashing golden in the dying sunlight. Before it hit the ground, Egg leapt up, grabbed it, and placed it safely back on Dilah's neck.

Carl roared in anger and frustration.

"Carl, it's over," Dilah said, his voice trembling but calm.

"What should be over is *you*! *I'm* the patriarch of the fox clan! The moonstone and the collar are both mine by right!" Carl fumed.

"That's why you did all those horrible things? How many of your fellow foxes have died because of your sense of entitlement?" Dilah said, his temper rising.

"In the face of the magic power of the Collar of Reincarnation, those things are nothing!"

"But what about their families? What about my parents? What about my brother?" Dilah questioned, his voice tight with emotion.

"Families . . . I wasn't even able to protect my own," Carl growled. "Why should I care about yours?"

"Why do you even want to be human?" Dilah pressed. "Is all of this really worth it?"

Carl barked harshly. "I curse my fate, curse the Arctic foxes! After all I've done for the white fox clan, the moonstone should be mine. I was their greatest warrior. But not only did I fail to obtain the moonstone—after losing my power, I was abused and trampled on by the other foxes, cursed and maligned." He paced back and forth, glaring at Dilah with his bright yellow eyes. "I promised myself that I wouldn't come back as an Arctic fox in my next life . . . In fact, I will destroy the fox race once I'm human!" he growled. "Once and for all."

Dilah nearly felt sorry for him.

Carl must've sensed his pity, because his next words were colder and angrier. "I'm better off than your father! He's dead, but I'm still alive! In the end, Gale defeated Blizzard!" Suddenly, Carl charged at Dilah with surprising speed. Dilah tried to jump out of the way, but Carl closed his teeth around Dilah's leg and hauled him to the edge of the cliff.

"Get off him, you big jerk!" Egg cried.

Egg wrestled Carl to the ground, and in one heartwrenching moment, the two of them tumbled over the cliff.

Dilah's bloodcurdling cry pierced the air as he watched one of his greatest friends and his bitter enemy fall to their deaths, Carl's fur like white snow fluttering in the darkening sky.

———◇———

Majestic Fox Mountain was shrouded in the scarlet afterglow of the setting sun, the distant sea stained red in the grim twilight. Dilah stood alone in the rubble, scanning the aftermath of the battle, the mountain littered with bodies. Blake. Warren. The two red foxes. The four Arctic foxes. The short man. Alsace, his brother, who he never had a chance to know. Little Bean. Tyrone. And . . . Ankel! Dilah stifled a sob as he caught sight of his dear friend, fallen along with the others. He hadn't seen him go. He wished he could have said goodbye to each and every one of them. Far below, hidden by the sea, Egg lay in his watery grave too.

"I'll see you on the other side, friends," whispered Dilah to the breeze.

Dilah wanted to cry. His whole body was covered in blood, his heart raced in his chest. But he knew his mission wasn't over yet. He limped up the neck of Fox Mountain toward the top of the head.

Dilah heard a cry from farther down the mountain. "It's over there!" The tall man who'd escaped was pointing up at him. He had three other men with him now, all armed with shotguns.

Dilah turned away and walked on, up between the two peaked ears, refusing to rush. At last, he arrived at the fox's giant protruding snout, which stretched out over the raging sea.

He slowly walked out to the tip of the nose, inhaling the salty air. He gazed down. The bottomless sea surged, a fitting resting place for the collar. No one would be able to find it there. Everyone who could have guessed at its location was now gone, and soon he would be too. His head was dizzy, his heart thumping. He stared into death's open arms.

"Master, do you really want me to sleep on the sea floor?" The little golden fox on the collar suddenly opened its mouth.

"Don't try to talk me out of this," Dilah said. "I've made up my mind."

"I'll only return," the little fox said. "And I'll never be forgotten."

The four men had followed Dilah right up to the top. Dilah turned around, met their gazes. One by one, they aimed their guns at him.

Now.

Dilah took a deep breath and leapt into the air, his

teeth clenched. He heard a burst of gunfire, felt a sharp ache. He'd been hit in the back, leg, stomach, and chest. But what did it matter now?

Dilah fell. The wind rushed in his ears. He no longer felt any pain. The fall seemed to last forever. His mind flooded with familiar images. His mother telling him a story in their den in the Arctic. Meeting Jens and Carl in the blizzard. The joy of Egg rescuing him. The mystery of greedy Grandpa Turtle. The surprise of discovering the secret of the moonstone for the first time. Meeting the family of the forest watchman and rescuing baby Leo. The strange hole in the tree where Ankel's family lived. Helping the wild horse Kassel. The rabbit clan's sacred tree and ceremony. The excitement and disappointment of meeting his long-lost brother. Makarov's ominous warning. Emily's smile as she distracted the hunter. The animal beauty pageant. Tyrone appearing in the mist. The fantastic journey in the enchanted forest. The hair-raising wolf chase. The all-knowing prophet Gulev from Prophet Spring Valley. Opal's viciousness and vanity in the small seaside town. The shock of meeting Egg again.

The anticipation as the five friends explored Fox Island. And finally, the thrill of wearing the Collar of Reincarnation, and the heart-racing battle . . .

Splash.

Dilah plunged into the icy water, sending up a snow-white spray. He sank deeper, and deeper, and deeper . . . Bubbles streamed from his mouth. Cold and dark wrapped around him like his mother's tail. He could no longer see his paws . . .

———◇———

He could feel his breath and heartbeat, hard ground beneath him.

He was standing in a dark country, the darkness thick as ink.

Then, a patch of light grew in the dark. It reminded him of when he was cold and hungry among the frozen pines and found the light from the forest watchman's little stone cottage.

Dilah walked toward the light. As he drew nearer, he realized it was emanating from a golden archway glowing in the darkness, containing a pair of intricate gates.

The archway itself filled Dilah with a sense of solemn awe. He wished Ankel were at his side, for the golden surface was engraved with strange, complicated symbols and stunning reliefs that he wished he had the knowledge to decipher. He recognized carvings of the shining sun and moon and stars on the left and right sides of the gate. A giant eye was embedded above the gate, staring down at him. A pair of golden human skeletons had been wrought into the gates, locked together in an embrace where they met in the middle.

The Gate of Reincarnation!

As Dilah approached the gate, the two skeletons turned their heads toward him, staring with vacant eyes at the collar around Dilah's neck. They opened their arms, and the gate creaked open. Dazzling golden light spilled through the crack, growing wider and stronger until Dilah had to blink back tears.

Countless glowing hands welcomed him on the other side. Beautiful, unfamiliar music poured into his ears.

Nervously, he walked to the gate and peeked through, his eyes narrowing against the brightness. *Wow.* It was as though he was beholding the entire universe: the sun, the moon, and the stars, all spinning and shining beyond the threshold. He closed his eyes and lifted the tip of his nose, smelling the fresh scent of flowers and grass, hearing the calls of birds, feeling the damp sea breeze. How was that possible?

Now he was totally surrounded by the light flooding through the door. Warmth and happiness washed over him.

Unexpectedly, his sensitive ears picked up the sounds of a human's cries. The voice grew louder and louder. A human woman's voice. She was crying out in pain. Her voice had a magnetic pull, luring him beyond the gate. He had to go! He knew that with sudden, unmistakable urgency.

Dilah stepped across the threshold, leaving the endless darkness behind him.